ISBN: 978-0-9936521-7-2

RHAEVE

∞ ∞ ∞ ∞

STILLMAN
WILSON

Rhaeve

This book is a work of fiction. Any resemblance to people, places or events is purely co-incidental. Names, characters, events and places are either used fictitiously or are the product of the author's imagination.

ISBN: 978-0-9936521-7-2

Table of Contents

RHAEVE

Characters as they appear:

Rhaeve - Daughter of light – Mother of change – Princess of Rha –She who sees without sight – Wielder of power to change

Thum - Loyal protector of Rhaeve. Woodsman

Thurma - Wife of Thum

Orca - Navigator of the Old Ones

Bhola - Black crippled Nodite

Feena - Wife of Bhola

Nodites - Pygmies

Milkathing - Goat-like creature

Feebra - Son of Bhareve by a rape of Northerners

Old Ones - Live in three arks in The Valley of Death. The 4th one lives in the garden

Marples - Keeper of the lake

Sagyr - Machine beast of Marples Tinkerman

Stormrider - Leader of Rhaeve's guard. First rider of the line

Fulfson - 4th braided rider of the line. Second in command

Thurtson - Young Rider—Single braid

Stoneson - Holder of the Northern Keep

Thumson - Strongest son of Thum

Ahpoo Tree - Tree of knowledge: without it wondering is more in order than true thought.

Circe - Feathered Serpent

Circle - Tree of life

Snark - Evil snake that Nodites need.

FISHFIND

"Washed up on the beach, she was," cackled an old fish hag.

"Just like all the other unwanted garbage. Just another mouth to feed... If you was to ask me." A small, dirty man said, to nobody in particular. A crowd of fish-folk gathered around the raft that had brought the child in with the last tide.

"Does anyone know of her?" asked a skinny youth, fingering the heavy gold chain around the sleeping girl's neck.

"Never her likes hereabouts. And I be oldster I be," said another. "The wood of the raft be zotic wood of the big sea. None like it this side of the deep. Zotic wood brings strange cargo. Some say it brought Rhanian Lords in the past... Some say..." The oldster continued, leaning forward with both hands holding tightly to his walking-stick for support, and sending a sudden kick at the youngster that was still fondling the chain.

"Don't be touchin that belongs not to yar, Fishrong. You be a dumb younger, with yar hand in the wrong."

"Yar... She be kin ta summon... Fishrong" a very large and angry looking youth said, striding menacingly towards the skinny youngster who scuttled away from the girl.

""Not fraid of yar, yar don't fraid me, Sharphook!" Fishrong challenged, but quickly ducked into the crowd...

The crowd laughed at the antics of the two youngsters.

The oldster leaned forward, holding himself from falling by holding both hands on his stout walking-stick. He dropped to one knee and examined the medallion on the chain. He spat in the sand, and then rubbed his hands in the sand, as if washing off something unknown and frightening.

A slight shudder and he regained his feet with the help of the stout walking-stick.

"Be it the golden sign?" asked a small brown mother, clutching her two children close.

" Aye... She be wearing the gold of the great ones," the oldster replied, shaking his grizzled old head as if in doubt of his eyes. "Her head be bald, and her skin be as copper, she be a trueman sure. Glad I be her eyes are closed. I not want to see them... I thinks. Never there be word of a she-child, all have been boy-childs, never a she. I be goin. Feared of ill-things, I be," said the oldster, hobbling away leaning heavily on his stick for support.

"She surely be a pretty child. Can't be mor'n twelve winters. Shame for a youngun as she be to face the Tree, not knowing our ways'n all..." A crag of a man addressed the crowd in general. A great ax held loosely in his right hand. He scooped the child up effortlessly with his other great hairy paw in spite of her heavy gray leaden cassock.

"Child's alive, takin her home to Thurma 'n that's what I be doin. Any argue?" Thum the woodcutter challenged, glaring at the small crowd. Not a murmur from the shopkeepers and fisherfolk that were gathered around, for the temper of Thum the woodcutter was known to all. Seldom to see, but when it did, even old Guildsmen walked lightly. It was said, that far in the past, even the Lord Finder had had occasion to walk around old Thum. A gentle bear of a man. All agreed Thum couldn't have been a better trueman, even if he had been browner. In spite of his harsh whiteness, a better guildsman had never lived in Fishfind. All agreed.

Even the small gnarled black lord of Fishfind himself.

Thum ambled off through the crowd. "Any claiming her, knows where I be. Tell the Finder I be bringing the child for a Guild Finding…When she be feelin up to it." Thum said, addressing nobody in particular as he trudged off crooning to the sleeping child. Thum and his wife Thurma were childless after forty winters of marriage. Many the night poor Thurma had cried herself to sleep for failing her man. And all to Thum's agony. Their natural time had run out for having a child of their own, as seventy winters was approaching for Thurma. Maybe the Old Ones had decided for a different kind of child for them, and if the Old Ones had decided so, no man had better get in the way old Thum told himself.

No guildsman entered the shadow without doing so in an armed party, and then they only did so along the edges when traveling northward into the towns of other trueman that lived in Westernest in peace with the Black Nods of Westernest. None ever traveled to the eastern side of the Shadow, for the wild yellow Dervisals killed all that they found on their lands. Fortunately the Shadow grew to the sea in the south, and ran all the way to the great ice in the north. The Shadow being two full days ride across, and a full moons ride from south to north, kept the nomadic killers at bay. The Dervisals feared the Shadow, for trolls and sagyrs ran wild in the Shadow. Some said that even the small black Nodites lived in the Shadow. And if they did it would explain why few war parties of Dervisals ever came through into the land of Westernest.

Old Thum had left the far northern lands of his fathers, the White Riders, when tired of war with the Dervisals. He had lived through the Westernest and throughout the Shadow, only taking the deadwood of the shadow in his cutting. Never a live tree did he take from the Shadow. Woodcutters that did--lived short lives going to their cutting, never to return.

Within a few weeks the child was moving around with her health restored under the loving ministration of Thurma.

Rhaeve had taken to the kindly couple as they poured love upon her. A love she had never felt in her thousands of years alone on the island of Rha.

"My girl is of noble bearing," Thurma would tell townsfolk proudly, "yet she is not too proud to help old Thurma with the chores, and she knows things about the garden that would make ol Garmer green hisself, he would be, by jingo."

But all knew that the Finders moon was soon upon them. And all knew that the Lord Finder would call the child to the Finding.

The moon was full in two more days and Thum was ordered by the Guild to bring the sea-child to the Guild Hall in time to question and prepare her for the test by tree and chain. The Guild Finding was heard by all, and the Findings passed down in full light for all to see and hear. This was the way of the Guild. One justice and hearing for all. This was due to the influence in the past by the Rhanian princes who came into the land of Nod and dwelt there for thousands of years. In the land of man, they walked no more, only memories remained of their great deeds, but where they walked, truemen remained and walked taller, because of the influence left behind in the teachings of the Golden Ones. Gold of eye and hairless, yet copper hued of skin from eons in the sun, they walked tall, and goodness and great deeds were spoken of wherever they traveled. But they traveled no more, and some say they never were.

THE GARDEN

The Feathered Serpent sat on the edge of the well and peered down into the Glowing water. "The light has gone out," Circe, the young Serpent told the Old One that lived in the garden's well.

"Impossible! I feel her life force, weak but not out. Worm there are times I can figure not your intentions. Why speak, if your words are false. Why speak such mischief?"

"I lie not to you revered one. I only test to see if you have contact and interest in life other than in this living-dead garden. It appears that you still have contact, but have you interest in continuing with destiny... Or is it your destiny to live in this place forever?" challenged Circe, sitting up prettily on the wall that circled the well. With determination the Feathered Serpent pulled a ripe ahpoo apart and daintily picked each kernel from the bleeding fruit, and popped each red kernel into an even redder mouth.

"Always has your tribe doubted us, and always has your tribe followed us through the universe…Always with doubt and angry criticism. Why do you not leave and go your own way?"

"You are our way, most Revered One," the Serpent replied.

"What is to be done about her who can see without sight, and touch without killing?" asked the Old One from deep within the glowing water.

"I am only your voice," the serpent replied, with small petulant lips pursed in thought.

"You and yours have always been my voice, but more than my voice, you have been me. For my touch is death to all that live."

"Now you are twisting the truth, Old One."

"How?"

"Your touch is life to much that exists, even to me. My life would soon shrivel and die if not for your touch."

"Yes. . . But that which I touch and it lives and thrives from touch--is me--and I am it. So I am only touching myself in different places, and becoming stronger and more at one with myself."

"Your logic gives me problems in defining it."

"Then don't define it, for it only needs to be in place to work properly, defining it will make it work no better, nor will the lack of conscious definition hinder it's process," came the thoughts from deep within the well.

"Do you seek to confuse and confound me?" asked the serpent slyly, flying up to pick a juicy golden fig.

"No, for I have small intellect, and without the great sight of the sleeping Mother, I am without purpose. You have the gift of abstract reasoning, and the potential for insight into the great plan. I am only the power that can help you achieve your very important possible destiny."

"If I am such a potential, how is it that I know nothing, and am able to figure out no escape to this situation we are in?"

"Because you are only an infant and must learn from your Great Mother that which will allow you to become as her."

"But She will not waken," mused the serpent.

"True... she has slept for long, and we are all in limbo until she awakens," rumbled the voice from deep in the well.

"Is that the purpose of the princess? Is she the catalyst that will awaken the Great Mother?" asked the Serpent, sucking greedily on an over-ripe apricot.

"You ask questions that I have no answers for, I too have many questions, I would give much of my power for just a small amount of intelligence and direction"" the voice bubbled up from the well.

"Why do you not come out of the well, then we could leave this garden. The fruit is delightful, but I grow weary of this place, I only have you for company, and company you are not. Why can't you come up and talk to me? Would that be so bad?"

"It would be certain death to you child, for my breath is death to all that live. Even to look upon me is to die horribly," the old one said, sadness in his mind-voice.

"What of the Mother?" impishly asked the Serpent.

"No, my life is her power to use. And she has left me in this garden and gone off to sleep in a desert surrounded by me without being me," bubbled from the well.

"Truly I can learn nothing from you, for you are insane, or just purely stupid. How can you claim to be trapped in a well, then claim that you are elsewhere near the Mother? If you are near the Mother as you claim, then get yourself out of the well and go to yourself. And become one with yourself, as you put it. I think you are crazy, and I am destined to live with a mad thing into eternity. This is not fair that I am destined to spend a lifetime talking to crazy bubbling water."

"Then fly away little one, and seek a better destiny."

"Fly Away! FLY AWAY!! You are truly mad. If I leave the sanctuary of this garden, all the kill-crazy creatures on this terrible planet will hunt me and kill me. They fear me and hate me. And for no reason. I've tried to leave many times, and they hunt me with sharp flying sticks. All the time screaming and howling how evil I am... Me!! I have not a mean thought for anything that lives. And they hate me on sight. And you say to me that I should fly away and seek my destiny... Madness is all around me!" The small feathered serpent complained, flying to a tree and hiding its bright green head under a violet wing.

It slept and dreamt of singing and playing with creatures like itself that had no sharp sticks, and sang sweet music.

From deep in the well the Old One felt sad for the misery of the young one, but knew no answer...

If only the Great Mother would waken from her deep sleep.

If only the experiment with the sea creature had worked.

If only she of the power that does not kill would come.

If only.

THE GUILDHALL

The Guildhall was a great natural cavern, large enough to accommodate more than twice the population of Fishfind. All the village was present, from the Lord Finder himself, deep in the recesses of the cave. He sat high on his raised stone canoe of truth. Only his canoe was upright, and of stone, all the others were used daily and stored nightly in the Guildhall.

The first row from the Finder belonged to the oldsters.

These great sea canoes were all hand carved, with the history of Fishfind proudly chiseled into their gleaming sides, for the children to see and know of their heritage, and deep ties with the sea and sons of the Old Ones. On the great stone canoe was the telling of the first great golden prince that landed and mated with a native before leaving north for the land of Nod. She died giving birth, but her son was the first to write the short genealogy of man at Fishfind. And that was a few thousands of years in the past. Each and every generation of man thereafter was carved in stone in the walls of Fishfind's Guildhall. The Great Hall of Truth was sacred to all. And on the canoe of truth itself was recorded the visitation of each and every golden prince who had come ashore over the years of Fishfind's history.

The final fan of diminutive, but functional canoes, belonged to the youngers of Fishfind. Children of Fishfind first learned to swim, then walk, and soon after to paddle. Not in toy canoes, but in seagoing canoes with the oldsters, then when reaching puberty rites they were given a position in a youngers canoe till the passing of twenty winters; only then with the final rites of manhood did they receive a seat in a great red canoe with the men. With the seat of manhood came the right to wife; then a hut was erected by all the women of the village in honor of manhood.

Ancient customs in the going-to-sea and in the Guildhall of Finding was serious business, and was in fact the very backbone of their lives, and it was not to be taken lightly by anyone. Not even by the smallest child. There had always been the sea, the Finding, and the tree. Only the chain had been changed from generation to generation. Some said that at a time in the past there had been no need of the chain. Those being tested by the Finding had stayed of their own free will at the tree. It could still be done in the old way, but nobody could be remembered to stay at the tree without the help of the chain.

The Finder sitting high in his stone canoe was resplendent in his great robe of white virn wool, holding in his left hand the Staff of Truth, cut in generations past from the living wood of the tree itself. In his other hand the white virn wool cap that would belong to the sea-child if she passed the test of truth. All present in the hall wore their hat of truth. Their hats were gray, not having been earned at the tree. Only old Thum and the Finder wore the white of Found Truth. The older a villager became the more respected he became for wearing the hat of truth. But all were open to challenge, and all could appear before the Hall of Finding, but to accuse was to be accused, and the accuser would also face the finder who sat in his totally unchallengeable seat in the great stone canoe. And many the final testing was put to the tree-and-chain, with both the accused and the accuser on the chain together for the final answer. The village lived in harmony with few wishing to take the tree as a final truth for being idle of mouth. Not even the Finder or Thum with their white virn hats were above being tested again by the tree of blind truth.

"I the Lord Finder of Fishfind bring this Finding to the sight and hearing of our village. Any present who have reason why this Finding should not be heard speak now or this Finding will begin, and it's outcome will be the truth for all to know" ….. The Finder stated to all those standing before him. None replied.

"So be it. This Finding will begin and not be finished until the Truth is heard by all. You will all sit and not rise until the Truth is heard by all present." So saying, the Finder removed the white cap from the Peg, and placed it on the staff, which he placed in the light-hole of the stone canoe. The white cap remained in sight all during the hearing, for all to see. All knew that from the Staff of Truth it would go to the head of the girl. . . Or back to its peg above the canoe.

The Finder asked, "What is your name girl?" starting the Hearing of Truth.

"I am the Rhaeve of Rha," Rhaeve replied simply.

"Of Rha? Come now child, Rha has long since ceased to be, other than on the walls of Fishfind, and in stories told at fireside. Even so, it has been over six thousand winters since a Rhanian prince landed on our poor shores. Never a princess, only princes have ever come from Rha. And it is all scribed in stone for non to challenge or change. Do you think us gullible child?"

"You call me child. I am the Rhaeve of all that came. I am the Rha-Eve of all True Men. Even you monkey-man, safe in your old blackness, are child to me. For your village was founded by a son of son on my day of one. Call me not child, small one, or child I will show you I am not. The Finding is your way, and I will respect it for the love shown me by Thum and Thurma," the strange child replied, a cobweb of gold showing in her sea-foam eyes, that she closed quickly, so non could see and fear her.

And so none would die a slow painful death.

"Well you reply... And I will grant you respect due to a child in a strange land," the Finder conceded.

"If I am unknown to all that gather at this hearing, it is only because this hearing is ill informed and walks in darkness."

"In darkness!" spat the Lord Finder.

"Yes, in darkness. Your village may be well informed in the passage of things here, yet you are merely the most informed of those that live in eternal darkness, those that begin to die, even as they are birthed. Sad it is monkey-man, but true. It is the way for man born of man. Man's way is the way of death. As he is birthed his days are counted on the small- days of life, and too soon he is recalled to the earth," Rhaeve said,

"We of Fishfind bear the royal markings and are the direct descendants of the first Rhanian princes that walked these lands."

"Yes, that is so, but when they reached your shores they were already far from the tree. Each prince born of a mother who died in his birthing. Each farther from the tree than his father. Each a death for his mother who birthed him, and a sure giver of death to his wife who bore his single male child. The Rhanian Line was a line attempted by the Old Ones to perpetuate their own Line. It was an experiment that failed. Failed miserably," the fragile girl told the crowd around her, looking at each of them in compassion for their shortness of life.

"And you know all this? And you know it to be fact child, your story is foolish. On our wall is the true writing of man from his beginning here at Fishfind. We have no recording of mothers dying at birthing. From the beginning of our time, as is recorded on the wall, mother's have born male and female children, and have lived after birthing. If what you say is true; then its truth in itself that is a lie. For if mothers birth only male children, how can you lay claim to being Rhanian and a girl? You are found to be liar by your own mouth. If your story be true and Rhanian mothers birthed only male children, then you are either a boy child... or liar. Methink LIAR!" The Lord Finder concluded, having trapped the child in her strange tale.

"I find you not guilty by my Finding and my word. No....I find you guilty and liar by your mouth." The crowd cheered for the clearness of mind of the Lord Finder. For all were fair and would not want to see a child go to the Tree if there was any doubt of fact or truth.

"Surely I am female. And surely I live. I am the Rha-Eve. I am the before of all who came, and all that left our shore, when the women of the Isle were no more. Then the Old One left with his serpent and there was no birthing on the Isle. I the Eve of all, being the only female life on the Isle of Rha. The teachings of the old ones forbid birthing between Rhanians. The purpose of life to come, according to law set down by the Old Ones, was for a son of the Old Ones to take unto himself a wife of man. This way, after repeated birthings a female child could be born, and the mother live after the birthing. Don't you understand?"

"Child, the only thing this finding sees and understands, is that you are a bright and imaginative child, but fools we would surely be if we believed that you... A child, could be Mother of all that came. If this be true, you are asking us all here, even to the oldsters, soon to die, at old age of l00 winters, to believe that you are thousands upon thousands of winters old. Do you expect us to believe this my Child?" the Finder asked, tired of the dragging out of a Finding already Found.

"I demand the right to address this Finding. I do not ask humbly, I demand, as is my right of the white virn hat I wear. Do any challenge my right?" Thum asked looking to the faces of all present. Some looked away, some looked to the Finder for counsel, and some looked to the floor. All agreed that Thum had the right to tell his story. None wanted to see the poor child face the tree. They believed her to be a poor sick child, and that was not good reason to face the tree.

It was mid-afternoon when Thum started his incredible tale, and it was deep into the night before being told. All agreed that the tale was too incredible in its complexity for a child to dream-upon-a-time. Even in its telling by Thum, the Lord Finder decided that the child was not trying to mislead the Finding. He decided for some unexplainable sick reason she believed what she said. Regardless, it was wrong, and she must face the Tree of Truth. For that was the way of the village.

"Who could ever be sure?" From the Finder.

"The test. The test." From each canoe.

All agreed to the test. And it was passed that the Finding would be found. If the child lived, her word would never be doubted again. It may not be understood the way of, but it would never be challenged or doubted again. For that was the way.

To the horror of Thum, he knew the child would have to face the test of chain and tree. Thurma broke into tears and Thum placed his great arm over her shoulder and patted her absent mindedly, as he was deep in thought.

"Worry not for the girl Thurma, for the Finder has the right to send her to the Tree, but the Finder has no say of the doings of Thum, and Thum will be there. Thum has no fear of that which kills only those on a chain. Not a bit," Thum told Thurma with deep anger in his voice. He ran his hairy thumb along the edge of his great sharp ax. "Trees fall before my great ax, and by all that's right and Holy, nothing is bigger'n trees. Nothing as tall. And they fall before the ax of Thum".

If only Thum was as sure as he tried to make Thurma believe. Black thoughts of terror and of an unknown horror seized Thum.

If he only knew what he would be facing, then it would not grip him so strongly. The tree and chain had been a way of life for thousands of years. Some said the tree and the town were as one, and only the chain was changed from generation to generation. The town knew the tree had always been, and always would be, and they knew it was the truth of the finding that kept their village civilized and gave equal justice to all.

"The Finder has the right to test the child with the tree, but law of the tree stops me not from watching the child. This be a small Finding of truth. Rhaeve will not have to be chained for more than one night and Thum be there. So dry those lovely eyes Thurma. Thum will be there," the old bear consoled Thurma. If only he felt as sure of himself as he led Thurma to believe. But Thum knew of all the accused that faced the tree, only he had not met the beast that feeds at night on the edge of the shadow forest. Only blood and gore had been found of all others that faced the tree. Always in a trail leading to the stench filled black hole of a cave at the base of Mount Fishwatch.

In mid-afternoon the whole village made the trek through the brambles and meadows and the young growth of trees to the edge of the Great Shadow itself. Great black-and-gray giants of trees as old as history rose to the skies... In the darkness of their tops, thick boughs intertwined like great brutal arms, and even higher above the arms could be heard feint and frightening voices, whispering of things unknown to man and foreboding in their strangeness to all that walked the soft lands below. None ventured into the Shadow near sunset. To be caught in the Shadow after dark was to be never seen again. Yet the legend was inscribed on the walls of the Guild Cave--that the great Forest had an affection for the westernesters of all villages, as they had never entered and killed any living tree. Only the Northern savages and the Yellow Dervisals had ever killed any of the great trees. But who could be sure? And the timid villagers stayed clear of the Shadow.

Less than a thousand steps from the horrible-hole at the base of Mount Fishwatch squatted the gnarled dwarf. Gray and lifeless, never a leaf or sign of life. But it lived and had lived from early history at Fishfind. Always the tree had existed as a living-dead reminder of Truth.

As soon as a child could walk it was taken on the trek. Each child was taught that lies causing evil for others could lead to being tested by the tree. Sometimes the Guild felt that the Finder created reasons for testing villagers--none voiced it openly, for fear of being next.

The Finder carried the Living Staff and his word was law. And the tree made the final decision. In their generation, only the Finder and Thum were Found Members of the Guild. Only they had survived a night at the tree. Many a night Thum would awaken in a cold sweat, not to sleep again that night. All in memory of his night with that terrible tree. The Finder had even more winters than Thum. It was said that he had endured two nights with the tree. And any man that could spend two nights with the tree was Found--never to be lost again. But only Thum had spent a night with the tree in the lifetime of the living Guildsmen.

The time had come, and in sadness the child was left chained to the tree.

Not one Westernester left the tree with a good feeling in their hearts, as to the outcome for the strange girl.

Rhaeve was happy that they had finally brought her to what she hoped would be the beginning of her journey into finding traces of where her people had all disappeared to. She could not believe that the males of her tribe had disappeared from the face of Rhapour. Somewhere on this planet she knew there had to be kinsmen. They could not have all been killed in wars while attempting to civilize the savages of Rhapour. As savage as Rhapourans were, they still were not any match for a Rhanian.

On not one of the planets that the old ones had tried to colonize with hybrids had they achieved any success. No, not one tribe that they had genetically re-engineered had developed into a tribe that could be introduced into the Federation of Warless States that dominated the Milky Way. Some of the Old Ones told of genetic journeys to other stars, but always with only failure to report to the Federation. Evolved man was always bent on insane, mindless destruction. Only the first few generations of trueman held the values of the Old Ones; then the violence of evolved man would dominate the offspring and darkness and violence would rule. Never a successful experiment. Yet for millions of years the old ones had continued tirelessly in their quest in the galaxy. As a child, thousands of years earlier, Rhaeve had sat at the feet of her- Gene Father and listened to his tales of endless defeat, and on Rhapour the experiment had been doomed before it started; the great pyramid had nova'd on the landing, killing all but four of the Great Ones, and they had been so badly disabled that they could not send a mind-probe for help. Even as mind-cripples they had tried their compulsive attempts at peace. Failure and aggression by the savages of Rhapour had driven them into hiding, and probable death. For they had the inability to kill--even in defense of their own lives. Rhaeve had been told many times at the oasis of Knowledge in the Garden that for an Old One to even consider the death of another living entity, would bring his own death. Empathically and with all the pain that can only be imagined in a nightmare, which is tenfold greater than any felt in a purely physical happening.

It was a gamble for Rhaeve to come to Fishfind. She knew beforehand of the tree and the monster that existed here. What kind of monster she had no   idea of....

THE TREE

Night came slowly, the tree being at the base of a mountain on the western side. Visibility for Trueman would be good, as the moon was full. For Rhaeve it was always light, for in the dark her nictitating membranes opened fully and her great eyes glowed from the moonlight certainly, but more from within. As quietly as a great water buffalo, Thum stealthily pushed and pulled and tore his way through the underbrush. Thum was creeping up on Rhaeve as silently as a mouse-- for a Trueman. For Rhaeve the racket was almost drowning out the other noises.

Rhaeve was forced to strain her concentration to hear the whimpering, the giggling. Then, she could make out a small angry voice coming from the forest. It was only one voice, but it was deeply disturbed with itself, and deeper yet in open aggressive conflict with itself.

Whatever it was: it was definitely very angry with itself about something.

The great beast stopped at the edge of the old trees. It stopped to mind-feel the pray. No fear. Thragg could feel nothing coming from the tree. He stopped and pulled a great bough down from above to shield him from glowing eyes that peered directly at him from behind the tree with the chain. Thragg had seen the black smoke from the Guild Hall. He knew that meant food was at the tree. Always after the black smoke came food to the tree. Thragg knew this, for he had eaten at this tree for a great many years. And always with the special black smoke from the Guild Hall came feeding for Thragg. Thragg was angry. He could not feel the thing at the tree. Thragg felt the other thing. He knew what that thing was. It was the thing with the Ax. Thragg didn't like the thing with the ax. He reached out tentatively to touch minds with the ax thing. Quickly he recoiled.

"What can this thing be?" Thragg asked himself.

""I don't like this thing. Go away thing," Thragg mind yelled at the thing with the axe, then quietly, Thragg mind listened to see if he was heard. Thragg heard mind laughter, then it was gone. Thragg quickly touched minds with the ax bearer. Recoiling quickly at the intense anger and desire to kill. And to kill Thragg! "This is not good. Go away ugly man," Thragg mind yelled, giving himself a slight ache behind his eyes. "Go away! Go away! Go AWAAAAY!" He screamed at the top of his mind, bringing such an ache to his mind that he let go of the branch and sat down against the tree to recover. When he could mind see again he peeked out carefully at the horrible white worm with the ax.

Thragg could feel the presence of the cave things. He knew that very shortly they would be coming to the tree. They always came. Thragg had to get to the tree before they did.

A stench of things long dead and left to rot assailed Rhaeve. But not from the beast at the forest end. No, this putrid, stomach-revolting stench came from the cave.

Rhaeve could feel the beast's concern for whatever was in the cave. Rhaeve sensed a deep need to get to her. And the need was to get to her before that which cringed in the cave did. From the cave came a totally unintelligent need for food. And the need came from many unminded creatures. Her mind-probe revealed nothing except angry fear. And that fear was being overpowered by the need to eat. She could read nothing more from the cave.

The beast started to move towards the tree. As it moved out into the bright moonlight, its shape could be clearly seen by both Thum and Rhaeve. Tall as a house, quiet as a mouse, it waddled like a great pickle, with little stubby legs, and long tree-like arms that hung nearly to the ground. As the great beast waddled toward the tree, it could be seen clearly, as the cloud cover drifted away, leaving the night as bright as day. It had appeared as a pickle from a distance, but now, seen in the bright blue glow of the moon, Rhaeve could clearly make out the strong white and black markings.

"May the great ones themselves protect us this awful night," Thum said to Rhaeve, as he stepped in between the great beast and the child. "By a dreadful, it be the king of all killers that ever swum the deep. It be the Great Orca himself... Come to land. Terrible it be that he fright all fisherfolk that travel the deep; by all that is terrible he has come to land to continue with his spread of terror."

Thum raised his ax high, but the huge orca was not coming directly at the tree. It had come to a halt, not fifty feet from the tree. From his great height he bent his massive head and opened his great mouth, displaying dazzling white teeth. "He means to eat us alive, "Thum told Rhaeve, his ax wavering from side to side, ready to fight the beast.

"He is smiling... He's happy that he arrived in time," Rhaeve laughed. "Come set me free, my gentle Thum."

"Arrived in time? Surely he's in time. He's in time for his supping. But a costly supping it will be. Thum's ax be sharp, and Thum is not to be tricked by no swumming thing that should be in the briny," Thum replied, never taking his eyes from Thragg.

"Come set me free. Get the key from the Guardian."

"You think it has a key?" Thum asked incredulously.

"I know he has a key. How else have all that been chained to this stupid tree been freed? Put down your ax and approach the orca with your hands held out in front of you."

"I'll not approach the beast without my trusty ax. I'd as like to fall on my ax. Child, I be glad'n proud a life to save you from this great beast, but dangum iffen I'll throw our lives away. No I won't throw them away. The beast may take them, but he'll nar get them without a price," Thum said with passion.

"Thum I want you to put your ax down of your own will. Don't force me to make you do it. He'll not trust you if I force you to put the ax aside. Walk to him as a friend. With both hands held forth in friendship."

"You frighten me when you talk foolish, child."

"I know. Good and brave friend. I know. But you must trust me...I know you love me Thum, and I love you and Thurma, but now you must trust me. Let me help you see the thoughts of the Guardian. Once you see his thoughts you will realize what I am trying to say," Rhaeve said, quietly and gently to Thum.

Thum held his ax tightly.

Slowly Thragg turned his back to the tree and faced the cave. Thum thought of attacking the beast from behind. But for some reason unknown to Thum, he was not able to move.

As the overhead moon reached its zenith, the second moon of Rha appeared on the horizon, giving greater light than the smaller overhead moon. With the second moon came the cave things. Howling slathering Tuskors. Fierce carnivorous Tuskors. They came for the tree as they always had done in the past. And the great Orca--Thragg was there to meet them, as he had for thousands of years. Thragg had absolutely no idea why he protected the things on a chain from the things in the cave. But he knew that it was a thing he must do! Thragg knew that this was not natural for him to be on the land. Thragg knew this was not his destiny to spend eternity watching this tree, but he could only dimly remember doing anything other than being the Guardian of the tree. Dreamily he thought of swimming in far off waters. Never a clear thought could he concentrate on. He knew that his purpose in life was to be something of greater value than to protect these pathetic creatures from the Tuskors. He knew that he was not to eat anything that lived. He knew that eating of meat of a living thing was wrong. But when he tried to reason why... the dream fog slipped across his mind, and he only could wonder why his destiny was to guard the tree. Thragg hated the terrible thoughts that the Tuskors pushed ahead of them as they attacked.

Thragg loved eating Tuskors. This was the first time that the thing on the chain had looked at Thragg without fear. She actually seemed to be waiting for him. He picked up muddled thoughts from the tree. Somehow those thoughts seemed barely clearer than his own... one thought came through very clear." She thought he was pretty. Hummmph!

Thum could not believe his eyes. The pack of Tuskors was attacking, as if they had no will, other than to attack him. And as they did they were snatched up by his great arms and thrashed against the ground. Soon the great beast was sitting on a huge boulder, happily munching on the Tuskors. With his huge hand he could flip a whole Tuskor into his cavern of a mouth then sit and chew placidly. Thum could actually see the contentment on the great beasts face.

"Mighty hard to hate the thing. Saved our lives he did true. And why do I know he be a he?" Thum asked Rhaeve.

"I told you that Thragg was a male. I also asked you to get the key. Put down your axe, and get the key. I am starting to understand why we are all at this tree."

"Child, strange things be about us here. Methinks strange things goin on since you came a Fishfind. Methinks moreover you never been a normal kinda prisoner. Methinks you never been a prisoner 'tall. Methinks. . ."

"Yes I see all those confused thoughts running through your mind. But I am a prisoner. I am a greater prisoner than you could know... Greater than I can know. But Thragg may have answers he knows nothing of."

"Child if he has thoughts he knows not. How be he tells you that which he not rightly knows?"

"There are ways. But never mind, that is my problem, and I see that you will not go to Thragg for the key."

"No. Mad you be. I'll stay by you child. Strange things about. Too deep for the simple of Thum. But ax is ready and willing."

The great orca having finished the last of the Tuskors wiped his lips and burped. Contented that there were no more Tuskors to eat, he headed for the tree, thinking happy, stomach full, thoughts. He hated the endless watching of the tree, but the eating was plentiful. If he could figure a way into the cave, then he would really eat up a storm... Ahh...

"Come no closer--Beast," Thum challenged.

"What a brave little man," Thragg boomed.

"Come closer, and feel the brave of my ax."

"Aha, a sense of humor. Good, good" Thragg boomed, showing his great white teeth in a grinning mouth, a mouth if opened any wider would cause Thragg to lose the top off his large domed head.

"Thragg, do you know who I am?" Rhaeve asked aloud, so that Thum could hear.

"No, but I know that you are the reason that I have been at this stupid tree for thousands of years. I know that I have been commanded to wait for her that can talk without words."

"Who gave you such a harsh order?" Rhaeve asked, feeling genuine concern for Thragg.

"Only dimly do I see within my mind, deep within the darker grays do I see patches of knowing, and they come and go, as if lights that are turned off and on for no reason… And never do I have control to keep them on. When I challenge too strongly—a harsh bright light sears through my head. Then I am left with less awareness of who I am than before. But always the one thought has remained constant. And that is to wait for the silent, talker."

"Yes I see this. You are now free to leave the tree. Thum I want you to chop this cursed tree to the ground. Then you will burn it."

"What of Fishfind?" Thum demanded.

"Fishfind will have to find some other way of controlling its laws and morals. There are better ways. And they will have to learn them."

"I'll not chop a living tree," Thum declared angrily.

"I see that I have a great deal to do. Some of it I know the right of, and some I am not sure. I have known for years that I must come to the tree. That I must help the mighty Thragg find his way. My task is of great importance only in the matter of causing others to fulfill their destiny. This I know. I know that I must free Thragg. The tree must be no more. That Thragg must mind link wherever I go. And I know not where to go.

This is all so frightening to know that things of great importance are resting on me and that I have no clear sight of any of these happenings. I see that I must find an old one that I can't look upon. I see a valley of meeting. I see a lake of wonderment. I see an old one in a garden, needing help... I see stone trolls, that can't think without... I see a small man... Marples...Ohhh,.. I am so......."

"She has fainted," Thum accused Thragg, as if it was Thragg's fault. "What can we do?" Thum continued.

"Well to start you can put down that ugly ax and let me unlock the poor child from the tree. Then you can chop the thing down. That's what WE can do to start."

"What of Fishfind? Tree is only law."

"A law that does not change to address the needs of those it is meant to serve is no longer a law. It is a chain that binds. Even as the tree would have been, if it had not been serving a greater purpose," Rhaeve explained to Thum, sitting up

"Why did you faint?" asked Thragg

"I did not faint. I used too much power. It is not uncommon for me, but I have learned to live with it. Sometimes when I move larger objects I sleep for hours. I do not faint. I only drowse."

"Drowse or whatever... It could be dangerous," Thragg said, looking worriedly to Rhaeve.

"Truly I am confused. It seems that someone in the far past gave this village a code to live by, that was only done so that if and when you finally arrived, I would be here to greet you. I think a very unkind deed it is that would send so many to death at this tree, just so that if you happened by, you would be found."

"No, it was a two-fold plan. Its primary concern was for the developing of a social structure that was benevolent, and fair. Fair to all... And it has been." Thragg thought it over.

"What of innocents murdered at this tree? If not for a great beastie to save all. All would be food for the filthy that lurk deep in such a terrible cave," Thum demanded.

"All civilizations have harsh laws in their infancy. If Fishfind had not the tree given to them; they at Fishfind would surely have developed their own brutal laws. Laws that would have included torture and death, with little sense of fairness to all. Look into your heart and think of the laws that you faced in the north, those laws that have caused you to move a thousand miles and settle in Fishfind because its laws have been fair .Tell me this is a lie……Well?" Rhaeve said grinning at Thum.

"Killings!" Thum Persisted.

"There have never been any."

"Then laws have been empty?"

"No. No, the laws have had great meaning. And I can see they have been a great success. They have taught these simple fisherfolk to govern themselves fairly. The fear of the tree has kept them in line and given them a guideline to follow. Would you rather have the laws that rule the lands from where you fled?"

"No. But of those chained? Where of them?"

"Thragg tells me they have been taken to the valley of the Glowing Lake. You will see, shortly a guide will be here."

"By magic?" Thum challenged.

"Not by magic, as none exists, only in the minds of men."

"What of Marples the Magnificent? What of this great wizard who lives in the Forbidden Valley. It is said he talks to a great black creature that answers all questions. It is said the black creature sits with its feet in the enchanted lake Rha-Adium. And it is further said that Marples sits with his mortal feet in the Lake of death and speaks in a language unknown to any. What do you think of this...Rhaeve?" Thragg asked.

"Do you know of that valley Rhaeve?" Thum asked.

"I know nothing of the valley. I only know that things are seldom as thought to be. All things upon a closer inspection seem to be different than thought to be. I know almost nothing, and this is all that I am sure of. The other thing that I am not sure of is the why of, or the way of... I am only sure of what I must do. And I must go in search of a lake, not a lake of salt, but a lake of clear glowing water. I know not why, but I know that I must do this," Rhaeve said, placing her small copper hand on the arm of her friend Thum.

"Then you are set on going to this Valley of magic? A place that can only be entered through a black gorge that has never had light of day penetrate its evil depths. Many have tried the gorge, only to be met by the demons that live in its dank and foreboding crevices. The valley is truly home to demons too terrible to conceive, yet you ask me to follow you into its gloomy darkness," Thragg said in interest, but without fear.

"No, noble Thragg, you are finished with your heavy responsibility. However, for me, it is just starting to unfold. I know that my journey is of great import. And I know that if I fail in my small part, a great fabric in things to-be will be badly torn. Somehow I know that a great accident has happened here in the past, and it must be set right so that a greater destiny of that which I do not presume to understand can continue. I know that though my part is small, without it the Old Ones will not fulfill their destiny. Even now I am starting to understand the tree and the village of Fishfind. It is only one of many puzzles that I must look into without knowing why."

"Are you saying that the history of Fishfind has been preordained, and that all that has happened in every detail was part of a great plan by the Old Ones?" Thragg asked.

"No, nothing in the universe is certain and absolute in outcome. But each tribe of man when placed within a certain beginning will react to the environment and circumstances that they are exposed to. I get the picture in my mind that the Old Ones traveled the stars, creating starts of different nature on each planet that was already populated by primitives, and then they left. It makes no sense to me, but this is the picture I see deep within me."

"And what do you see for me?" challenged Thragg.

"Ah, your part is easy to read noble Thragg, would all that I must know be so easy," Rhaeve said kindly.

"Is my life to be known to me, or is it a secret that you will not share with a dullard such as Thragg. After all I am only a dumb creature born of a lowly water creature. How could such as Thragg play any part in such a great game as that which the Old Ones seem to be occupied with. If there still be any Old Ones other than at fireside, spoken of softly and fearful like, by hungry men, that be fearful of that which they do not understand,

and I think that is almost, everything they see."

"You are almost right Thragg, I do not believe the Old One has specific plans for you now that you have given me direction. Direction that I needed badly. You have performed a great task and I feel that in the future you will perform the greatest service that they have ever required," Rhaeve said, touching Thragg's great hand.

"What of Thum and all that live in Fishfind?" Thum asked.

"Fishfind has never been interfered with by the Old Ones. Why can't they now continue the way they have lived for thousands of years? And now they have an opportunity to take a giant step forward making their own destiny. If they have a good leader with good intentions, and good laws to guide them, why can't they continue in the light of day, with each man being his own man? I know you could be the first leader of a free Fishfind. And I see it to be your destiny. Go now before a Sagyr comes. I feel the presence of the demon coming for me. . . Go. You will make laws and find a way. It is clear to me. Go," Rhaeve ordered with her voice cold, and her mind clear. Tears running down her small coppery face. Just for a moment Rhaeve could feel the terrible empty agony of her fathers, and then it was gone. She knew that she was weeping as much for the emptiness of the Old Ones as much as she was regretting the parting with the gentle but brave Thum.

"Will Thum be able. . ." Thragg, started to ask.

"Thum will be fine," Rhaeve replied, dreamily.

"What of the tree? What of the laws?" Thragg asked.

"He knows the tree must be removed. I see in his mind a plan is already forming."

"That is good, but what of the laws? Without the laws to guide them,

Fishfind will slip into savagery,"
Thragg argued.

"I have given him the mother of all laws. I have given him the One-Law that all others grow out of."

"And that is...?" Thragg mind linked, trying to peek into Rhaeve's mind. Rhaeve laughed aloud.

"Commit no act that you would not have done to you. And by the way-- that covers you trying to trespass uninvited beyond my mind shield just now... You rascal," Rhaeve laughed, shaking her small finger at Thragg.

"The Old Ones usually start most primitives with at least ten very defined commands......" Thragg started to say.

"And how do you know this?-- Thragg!" Rhaeve cut in.

"Hmmmmnn......." Thragg looked deep into his own mind, looking for the answer, he found none. But he did see Rhaeve moving through his inner thoughts, delicately, but there.

"You just broke the law yourself," Thragg challenged, laughing and shaking a massive finger at her.

"Yes, I see that my kind is more inclined in creating laws, than obeying them... Ah well." Rhaeve reflected, leaving Thragg to his thoughts. . . For a while. . .

A STORM

A whirlwind of dust could be seen several miles away as it approached slowly. The great cone of dust swirling high along the edge of the Shadow Forest, suddenly changed course and headed across the black sands of the badlands, toward an outcropping of quartz rock. It was out of mindreach for Rhaeve, and she could get no imprint.

Small rooster tails of dust headed due north, away from the whirlwind, and also away from Rhaeve and Thragg.

"Ho--the Dervisals want nothing to do with the Sagyr," Thragg boomed aloud, laughing with great mirth.

"How is it that you can see at such a distance, yet your strength is not great. Not even strong enough to force a peek, or issue a command," Rhaeve speculated aloud.

"Powers come in different shapes and sizes--it would appear my small friend. For me the farther I see--the clearer I see. Not with power, only with clarity." Thragg replied.

"I wonder the purpose to such a strange talent. What could be the value to see that which you could not touch or control," speculated Rhaeve, looking to Thragg in wonder. Rhaeve knew that if she had the answer to Thragg--She might better know herself.

"Could it be just a wild talent that has no purpose?" Thragg asked, looking within for an answer.

"No, I think not. It is not the way of the Old Ones to be in need. And I know that they are deeply concerned for you."

"How can you tell this to be correct?"

"I can't be sure why, but I am."

"Makes little sense."

"Maybe we are not equipped to see the obvious."

"Maybe," Thragg agreed, but with little conviction.

The great sand spout moved up and through the outcropping of quartz. The spout formed a cloud and rained down on itself, and then the sky was clear. Slowly the spout rose in all its power and moved slowly towards Thragg and Rhaeve.

"The sagyr just convinced a small band of hostile Dervisals that to head north would be wise," Thragg told Rhaeve.

"I thought the Dervisals never cross the shadow," Rhaeve said.

"They don't. They must be crossing the ice to the north of it, then travelling along the white river."

"But that takes them through both the land of the White Riders in the frozen north, and then they must travel a thousand miles through Nod, along the banks of the White River... Why would they do this? There is nothing for those evil creatures here in Nod.

Only death awaits them at every turn," Rhaeve continued.

"Could it be, they like the rest of us, are not the masters of their own destiny. Could it not be that destiny itself is calling these warriors forth," Thragg speculated.

"If it is, it is not a destiny that I am to enjoy," Rhaeve told Thragg, thoughtfully. The tornado was quickly approaching. At the base of the funnel could be seen the cause of the twister. It was easily a fifty foot cat, with the neck of a great snake, ending in four terrible single eyed slathering heads, hissing and spitting, and showing jaws large enough to tear an armored war-horse in half with one rendering of those terrible curved teeth.

The sagyr sat on its haunches. All four eyes closed. It was fully five hundred feet from Rhaeve and Thragg.

"What is expected of us?" Rhaeve asked Thragg.

"First we must let it settle down, then we can approach it," Thragg replied.

The whining and snarling stopped, and the twister collapsed, raining sand and small bushes, rocks, even small dead animals in a fan pattern directly to the north of the sagyr.

The Sagyr sat and purred a slow terrible growl.

"The sagyr wants us to approach. Have no fear Rhaeve, it will not harm you. As a matter of fact its sole purpose is to protect and transport you, or, whoever was at the tree. You will be the sagyr's last mission from the tree. I will miss you, small one."

"Miss me? What do you mean? You are the only positive task that I see ahead of me. I have many to do, this I am sure of, but you are the only one that I know exactly what is demanded of me. How can I leave you? You will come with me Thragg."

"Do you threaten me child?"

"No, I only tell you that what must be is beyond our understanding. And moreover it is beyond our tampering with. And where I go. You go. It is that which must be. No, I do not threaten you good friend, I only speak aloud our common destiny."

"What if I disagree... And refused to travel?"

"There are no what-ifs for us Thragg."

"Do you have the power to command me?"

"Yes I have the power. The right I am not so sure of. Actually I am commanded from within to bring you with me. This is a doing that I have no control over."

"Prove this to me, and I will follow you without reservation. Even into the face of the death I will follow you gladly."

"And if I can't prove this to you?" Rhaeve challenged quietly.

"Then I will follow anyway.., But with reservations, not mistrust, just reservations," Thragg replied, just as quietly.

"I'm going to look within in search of a way of proving my quest," Rhaeve told Thragg. She closed her great seafoam eyes, and her breathing totally stopped. After a period of five minutes Thragg was starting to show concern.

"My mind shield is down Thragg, come link, and look into my depths," Rhaeve said, opening her eyes.

They stood facing each other. Thragg, from his great height of over twenty feet, Rhaeve from her scant five foot level.

"No. No, I will not intrude upon you little Princess. I see even from the outside of your shield traces of the power only the Great Ones wield. And never could this power be used for other than good. I will follow you into the mouth of death, if you ask it."

"Do you not find it unfair to you, that I am able to see your inner self, yet you in turn are not permitted to look into me in return?"

"No. For longer than it is possible to remember, I have been at the beck and call of the Old Ones. And they have never explained their reasons. And I have never followed them with anything in my mind but trust. I feel the presence of the Old Ones in you. I ask only one thing of you. It is not a demand, just a simple request. My mind is so empty. And I am deep in wonder of what I am--who I am--why I have been the Guardian of the tree for almost ten thousand years. I see none of the answers by looking within. My request is simple. Could you not look within for me and give me some answers to these questions. I only ask you to let me know the reasons. Only if I am permitted to know by the Old Ones. I do not mean to overstep the bounds of what I should or should not know. But if I am allowed to know of my purpose here... what is the harm in telling me?" Thragg asked.

"There is no harm, and I have already looked deep into your darkest recesses. I see a tunnel. . . An almost fathomless tunnel. Empty of imprints, as if your mind had been washed clean of almost all experiences. I see clearly your guarding of the tree to the point of losing your mind. I see a strange contact with four bright beings; too bright to gaze upon. In these lights I see only blindness, insanity, death, but no evil. I see a shimmering lake of light, with you and a great beast swimming in it together. And above all, I see endless star patterns forming, dissolving, and reforming differently. The other images come and go, but the star patterns are strong and fill your mind. Yet I see no understanding of them in your mind anywhere. Your only clear thought is being directed by a creature of light to guard the tree. That is your only clear thought," Rhaeve mind told Thragg, sitting down on a rock--exhausted.

"It is as I have thought all these years. I am somehow linked to the Old Ones, and their star travel," Thragg said.

"Are the lights in your mind the Old Ones?"

"Yes," Thragg replied, simply.

"Have I helped you know who you are?"

"No. Not who I am. Or even what I am. But at least I know that I am not crazy, only part of a great plan that may never have been clear to me. I feel that my part is of importance, yet I feel that I don't have to understand it to do my part in this unknown task."

"Then it seems we are the blind traveling with the blind on a quest, the direction and reason of, we can't begin to imagine the purpose of. The only imprint that is clear in my mind is that three of the lights are out, and the fourth is very weak, and if we do not get to it. It soon will exist no more." Rhaeve told Thragg wearily.

Where the Sagyr had sat, now existed only a great willow tree. It grew on a circular mound at least fifty feet in diameter. Its elegant vine-like branches spread in a fan that touched the mound all around. Inside the vines in cool dimness could be seen a small fountain bubbling temptingly

From deep within the bowels of the thing a deep growling issued. Rhaeve put her head to the ground to see if she could see deeper into this apparition... Nothing.

"What is expected of us?" asked Rhaeve.

"The only thing that has been expected of me in the past is to take the person from the One Tree to the sagyr, then go back to my pond by the Shadow. The pond has little food. Enough to keep me alive and hungry... Always hungry. Hunting on the land is not easy for me. Fortunately a good feed lasts me months."

"Your answer fails to answer my question, but as to the killing--I do not think you should kill to eat Thragg."

"If I do not hunt... How do I stay alive?" Thragg questioned.

"You have flat teeth Thragg. Flat. Not pointed. Big flat teeth for grinding grains. Who knows. . . Could your eating the wrong foods cause your mind to malfunction? Thousands of years of eating the wrong elements could affect your basic metabolism, changing you into something you are not. I am not saying this is so, but you do have big flat teeth. And thousands of years."

The sagyr came to life with a growling and once more a great terrible cat was sitting where the friendly oasis had been.

"What is it doing?" Rhaeve asked.

"It has never done this before. I don't have any idea what it is doing. Can you stop it Rhaeve?" Thragg replied.

"It is not a living creature. I can't even scan it," Rhaeve told Thragg, as they watched the sagyr quickly move out into the badlands, creating a greater tornado than it had arrived with.

"For something that is not living, it sure appears angry. What do you make of it Rhaeve?"

"I have no idea, other than I felt something trying to scan me, and I drove it out. Not gently I'm afraid."

"It's just a machine. I've scanned it many times. Why would it take offense to you scanning it?"

"I don't understand what you mean by machine, Thragg, but whatever it was, it was not a living creature. I can read all things that live. And I don't understand things that think without living."

"Well I hate to tell you princess, but most things that function in the universe are not living things by any standards you would know. This is one of the few places in the universe that has intelligence without machinery."

"And how do you know this?" Rhaeve asked.

'I don't know, but just being near you brings things to my mind. I know nothing of the how, but I do know that I know things that I didn't, just hours ago..."

"Well you can't be getting this information from me, as I have never been anywhere other than on Rhapour." Rhaeve replied.

"Could be you are awakening powers that have been sleeping. For example: I know that I can't go on the journey with you. Without radioactive water I would die. The pond I live in is mildly radioactive. And the great glowing lake in the valley of the Magician is highly radioactive," Thragg told Rhaeve.

"Then I will go without you, but I will return for you."

NOD

Rhaeve followed the dried up river bed for two days, facing broiling sun and freezing nights. Her great, leaden cloak, and hooded cassock growing heavy in the cold of nights-- too cold.

Then came sandstorms so great that Rhaeve was deprived of sunlight for days. . . Weak and freezing to death Rhaeve crept into a cave, seeking warmth and escaping the bitter, sand-driven-winds.

The cave floor was well-worn, but a quick scan assured Rhaeve that it was empty. She noticed that countless small fires had been used to cook with. Searching throughout the pitch black cave she found a small pile of faggots ready for firing, but she had nothing to start a fire with. High up in a wall of obsidian glass, black and smooth, too smooth to climb, Rhaeve could sense a shelf.

With her last energy she pulsed one last surge and projected herself to the shelf. Exhausted, she slept deeply, as deeply as she had on the Isle of Rha, and she slept deeply for a hundred years, untroubled and unbothered.

Bhola-the-lame was born with a club foot, a twitch, and a cataract in one eye... His mother died in his birthing. Shunned, but not cast out of his Nodite squata he grew tall...

In Bhola's 12th winter he was fully a foot taller than any male member of his squata. He was a giant by Nodite standards. Bhola-the-lame was five feet tall, and even if his other deformities did not mark him as being gugu to the squata, his height was ugly to all. All except Feena. Feena had been without a man since the three great White savages had raided her squata ten years earlier. Feena had been a young woman of fourteen winters, and ready for coupling with a man. The savages ruined her chances of ever having a man. She had been bedded constantly and vigorously by a huge, hairy, red devil. Although Feena had fought him strenuously, Feena had secretly enjoyed his manhood.

The White Riders had been slain while sleeping. Their mighty horses had supplied the small squata with dried meat that lasted until after Feena bore the large, hairy offspring of the Rider.

None would cast the first stone, and Feena and the red devil-brat lived unmolested in the squata. Life was miserable for the young mother, but she learned the ways of grubbing and growing. She even kept one spotted milkathing. It was a small scruffy beast, but hardy.

Now, Bhola-the-lame was coming into manhood and Feena had hopes. She knew that no squata maiden would claim a cripple such as Bhola... His size alone would have deprived him of a mate.

And his male bigness was a constant reason for laughter. Bhola was the only male in the squata that wore a loin cloth. He did this so that little children and old crones would not poke him with a stick and laugh at him. Feena found his male bigness interesting. She remembered the great red savage, and not always with regrets.

Bhola had always brought small bundles of faggots to the cook-fire, many a pouch of beetles, and occasionally a small animal that he had hand trapped. Bhola could find roots and water spots as cleverly as any of the elders. But Bhola-the-lame he was born, and Bhola-the-lame he would die.

Bhola reached his manhood and there was no hut for him in the squata. He wandered far in search of a place to build. Now that he was a man he was no longer welcome at the women's fire.

A mist was drifting from the Shadow across the badlands, with the mist came a great mindless stone troll. Squatting down beside a masqet bush, Bhola watched with curious fear as the great stone-beast lumbered in his direction, but with years of inbred patience, he moved not an eyelash as the great troll passed. His lack of involvement was not to avoid being seen by the troll, his stick-like stance in the sparse shadow of the masqet bush was to conserve body fluids. He would not move until nightfall. And just possibly a hop-along would seek the shade offered by the masqet, then he would have fresh meat to take to Feena. The troll stopped suddenly and turned and appeared to be looking directly at Bhola. Bhola was not concerned, he would wait for a few hours and see if the troll sat itself down, then Bhola would creep over and sleep in the shade of the always cool, stone thing. Bhola knew that a stone-troll that could be bothered to sit would stay that way for months. He hoped that it would sit, then the Dervicals that wandered in small hunting parties would leave the area in terror. Bhola had no fear of them, as they were too stupid to read the signs in the badlands.

Bhola sensed, rather than felt the approach of a snark. He knew it was coming for the shade of the masqet. He contained his growing excitement, for the snark would feel his body presence if he was not careful, then the snark would be the hunter, not the prey. Bhola could feel its presence as it was now only feet away, moving slowly and cautiously. The snark was the greatest taker of life in the badlands because of its highly potent poison. It was hunted energetically by the Nodites, for that same poison was the sole defense the Nodites had against all the other tribes. The snark was both their worst enemy, and their best ally against the large stronger tribes.

The badlands belonged to the Nodites and the deadly snark.

The snark came up out of the sand, inches away from Bhola. With a lightning movement the snark struck! But Bhola had anticipated the move and had the poisonous snake just behind the head. A quick bite with his small sharp teeth and the snark was dead. In the eternal struggle between man and snake, the first to strike was not always the winner. Quickly Bhola milked the fangs of their precious poison, then Bhola skinned the snark.

Happily Bhola headed for the squata with over seven pounds of valuable meat. Feena would be proud.

A swirling of sand told Bhola that a major twister was in the making, and it could blow for a full moon if it was a big twister. Bhola knew the cave was only a short distance away. Bhola knew it was gugu for his tribe to enter. Bhola also knew that if he didn't make it to the cave, he would die in the slowly developing twister. With no choice but death before him, Bhola entered the forbidden cave of darkness.

Time went by slowly for Bhola as the cave was blackness. But it was cool, and Bhola had never felt such pleasure in just laying on the sand. Precious moisture was absorbed by his emaciated corpse-thin body. Bhola dug deep in the moisture of the floor... Water! Life giving water...

Bhola knew that he had found a future for Feena and the red brat. Water in the badlands was a richness. Water was life. . . with it they could grow a garden, and even raise more than one little scrawny milkathing.

Surplus water to trade with. Bhola knew that his future was going to change. And if he only knew how much he would have fled in terror. Terror of the unknown!

Bhola and his new family moved to the cave. The squata was glad to see the end of all three of them. While none of the life conscious Nodites would throw the first stone of death; none were happy to have these three in the squata. To celebrate the going of the threesome the squata gave them a pregnant milkathing.

An uneventful trip, and they arrived at the cave. Feena hated the darkness of the cave, and immediately set about nagging Bhola into lighting the cave. Regardless of the quantity of pitch-cones Bhola and his little family toted in their wicker baskets, the cave remained dark. But at meal times it was bright and cheery.

Then Feena noticed the ledge.

They dragged sticks from the floor of the Shadow Forest, and bound them together with vines. Soon they had a ladder.

"Bhola, could we be doing something wrong?" Feena asked, years of conditioning overcoming her curiosity.

"No Feena. You have driven us hard to make this ladder. Now it is time to use it," Bhola argued determined to climb up to the ledge. Ever since entering the cave, Bhola had a feeling of not being alone whenever he entered the cave. He had never felt threatened, but for Bhola this meant little, as his life had been one of constant threats, so a non-aggressive threat meant nothing to him. Only the aggressive threats did he heed.

Bhola climbed the ladder!

"There is a sleeping child! Come help me."

"Could it be dangerous?" asked Feena suspiciously.

"Let me see! Let me see..." Feebra demanded excitedly, clamoring up the ladder, almost destroying it with his clumsy eagerness.

"What is it? What is covering it? It is heavy. Heavier than a rock," Feebra exclaimed, pulling the hood from Rhaeve's head.

Rhaeve had grown long brown mossy hair.

"It's a girl-child. Not biggern me!" Feebra yelled down to his mother who was already climbing the ladder.

The threesome worked tirelessly in cutting Rhaeve free from her leaden garments. Never before had she been free of them. Her shaven pate had sprouted a moss brown head of hair that reached to her knees. Her warm copper-hued skin had become white and sickly.

"Does her heart beat?" Bhola asked Feena, who had her ear to the child's frail chest.

"No--She be dead. Why has she not rotted?" Feena replied in wonder, opening Rhaeve's eyes, one at a time to seek some sign of life. Only orbs without pupils stared vacantly from the deep hollows of Rhaeve's oversized eyes.

"What can she be, that she lives not, yet she is not rotting away? Could she be the reason the cave is gugu?" Feena asked.

"I think she is not properly dead," Bhola answered.

"Well she is not properly alive!" Feena replied.

"Why do we not drag her into the sun, where we can better see her? In the dark we could miss something to tell us the way."

"Yes, into the sun" Feena agreed, not wanting a dead creature in her home. Rotting or not.

The sun was high overhead, baking the badlands, drying out and taking the life force away from all things fragile.

Rhaeve was the same height as Bhola, and after a hundred years without sustenance she was no heavier than the seventy pound stick-man. They carried her out easily and laid her gently in the bright sunlight. The milkathings both came over and gently licked her face.

"She be surely a girl-woman," Feebra laughed, getting a sound swat from Feena for his rude way of expressing himself.

"The sun is the life giver to all," Bhola told Feebra.

"Only plants and things of the earth," Feena corrected.

"Who knows what the sun gods do," Bhola said.

"Who knows why a tiny seed becomes a mesqet. Your mother be

right, but the ways of the gods are not known to us."

The hard sunlight beat down, warming Rhaeve. Her hair started to slowly change from moss-brown to a honey-brown, the maggoty whiteness of her skin was becoming pink from the intense desert sun. Bhola felt the sleeping child's chest. It felt warm and alive. He put his head to her chest to listen. He felt a sense of life. And this fleeting of life-force had saved him from many stealthy attacks by snarks in the past. Bhola knew better than to question his inner voice. Without it he would have long since fallen victim to badland predators.

"This child is alive!" Bhola told Feena.

"Alive! Don't be fool, Bhola. Too many moons have you walked in the sun without covering your head. Sun sickness is your reason for talking such fool talk," Feena chastised.

"Fool I be, but the girl lives…"

"Look... She be changing color," Feebra piped in.

Bhola took Rhaeve's hand to examine the changing color. He felt the strange excitement of holding something powerful that is sleeping, soon to waken. It confused him but he was not frightened. A voice spoke in his head, telling him to take all living things quickly into the back of the cave.

Born of the badlands, where no move should be made until the right time, then it had to be a lightning one, or death would be the outcome of slowness. The little family quickly dragged the two milkathings into the back of the cave, where light could not penetrate.

THE GARDEN

"The Rhaeve is alive!" shouted the Feathered Serpent into the well, fluttering around happily in the air.

"Yes. Yes. I can feel the force. She is drawing power. It would appear that she has removed her shield and is drawing direct power."

"Can she handle it?"

"It grows stronger by the second," said the Old One.

"Yes, even I can feel the power surging, but can she handle it? That is what is important. You still have enough power to remove us from this garden. Yet, you have not enough control to move safely. Will she control her power or will it control her as yours does?" asked the Serpent.

"Time will tell little companion."

"You are always telling me time will tell."

"And it will," calmly replied the Old One.

"Well it is telling me nothing, and I am sick of being trapped in this garden. You would sleep forever if let you."

"Yes that is your purpose. Mine is going slow, and yours is choosing our direction, little one."

"I choose to find the other Old Ones."

"You always choose company to isolation." came the musical voice from deep in the well.

"And little chance I get. We have existed in this garden for tens of thousands of years... Why?" came bitterly from the small unhappy, feathered creature.

"Because our family suffered a terrible accident long in the past. It was so long ago that your mother was young and full of life. She tried hard to free us from this planet, but the great Navigator was badly damaged, and only he sees and knows the star coordinates."

"Could my Mother not heal the Navigator?"

"No... Even your mother has not enough power left to heal the Navigator."

"Could you and the other Old Ones not supply her with the power? You still have powers that you try and hide from me."

"Nonsense! I hide nothing from you little one. You are young and know not the way of power... As mighty as you think I could be if I were to wield it. If I wielded it, this planet would be a wasteland in minutes," came the tired and almost defeated voice from the well, the music in the voice gone.

"If I had the power, I would get about doing things."

"Yes, and that is why I transfer no power to you yet."

"Am I ever destined to have even enough power to protect myself from these terrible creatures that imprison us in this garden?" asked the serpent with just a trace of anger.

"You are destined to wield as much power as you have the common sense and ability to control. And this does not include taking revenge on the natives for trying to kill you. They know not our ways, and to them you are a frightening creature, for you are certainly your mother's daughter. And she is awesome in her beauty... But she does frighten all who do not know her. She is a loving and gentle Mother, yet she terrifies all that she is thrust upon."

"What good is power if you can't even defend yourself with it? You must live in this hole in the ground, afraid of harming life forces lesser and of no consequence," argued the serpent.

"Until the answers to the questions you ask are second thoughts and in fact, mandates of conduct, you will have little power to wield my child."

"Can you not call the Rhaeve to free us?"

"First we must see if she lives or dies with such a terrible saddling of energy. She has shifted her draw to a distant star."

"Why?" from a disinterested small voice.

"Because she wants not to set the environment into unbalance by tapping too hard on this planet's sun. It is the natural use of energy that marks her different from you... That is why she already has shut down and you are not even given primary control over minor energy from your Mother."

"My Mother has slept for an eternity. Who will give me power? You are so unfair. You keep all the power and keep me a prisoner," complained the Serpent.

"When you show in your deeper self that you can handle power wisely, and with consideration for all life then you will have more power than you can possibly ever want," said the Old One.

"Who will give it to me? Not you… I can see that you think I would not be fair with it."

"Would you prefer to be with your Mother? She has been asleep for long, but with the awakening of a Rhaeve many changes will be coming. The Rhaeves in the past have always brought new life to us Old Ones, as you call us. In truth we are not old, nor are we new, we are in a state of constant change."

"Other Old Ones may be, but all you do is sleep in that hole in the ground and grumble about me," replied the serpent angrily.

"You are my eyes, my voice and most of all you are the intelligence that should guide me. I am only the power."

"If you are only the power, why do you not obey me?"

"Because I am only the power of right. When it is wrongfully directed I will not lend it to the doing."

"In other words, until I think the way you want, I will just be a flying feathered thing, with not even one of my own kind to enjoy life with."

"If it appears unfair now, when you grow up you will find company in all that lives. I delight in the living trees and plants of this garden... And I am in constant communication with all living creatures that live on this planet."

"You communicate with all living things?"

"Always. To lose contact would be a living-death for me."

"Then you are not trapped here?"

"Never." came the reply from the well.

"Then only I am a prisoner... Unfair it is!" howled Circe.

"You are only a prisoner of your own mind."

"You mean that if I could devise a way to leave, it would be possible for me to go from this place?" challenged Circe.

"It has always been such for all living things. And even more for you, as you are the inheritor of the voice... You are the only daughter to the Sleeping Voice of the Universe. Your Mother is the representative and controller of the one True Confederation. You are her only daughter."

"I understand none of this! If I am such an important member of the confederation, they are not showing it leaving me here."

"We are all victims of an accident until the Rhaeve finds a way to free us all. Without the coming to power, of the Rhaeve we all have had to accept destiny. Your day will come small one, but until you are large enough in menta-stature to wear the cloak of Authority you are committed to the garden. To leave it before your time would be to go to your death. The same lingering death that awaits me. You should be with your mother, so that you can properly develop and become what is only possible for you to be. You want petty powers now.

Well the power is not to be given ever..."

"Not to be given ever?"

"No. . . Power can't be given."

"How does it come?" inquired Circe slyly.

"You must be able to handle it before it comes to you, little one. And when you can handle it, it will be there for you. As this is the way of it."

"I want my mother... It is not fair!" howled Circe.

TO FISHFIND

From deep within the cave, terrible thundering followed each blast of lightning, then there was silence.

"Bhola, what can be happening?" Feena asked, not expecting an answer, just wanting to hear his voice.

"Great things are about us Feena. Hold tight to Feebra, and I'll go and see. The noise is gone. Never has the quiet been so strong," Bhola said quietly.

Bhola crept as only a dweller of the badlands can.

"Who are you?" Bhola asked the naked girl that stood facing the sun, with both hands held high. As if in salute.

"I am The Rhaeve of Rha. The Voice of the One Mother. Daughter of Light. I am the True Bringer of change. And you are the liberator of all that will be. You and your tribe will ever walk in peace and prosperity little one." Rhaeve said smiling kindly to the stick-man.

"Bring your tribe from the cave. Fear me not, for from this day forward your life will change. I am The One that interferes with that that is, and creates that which could be. Go bring your woman and the child. Bring the milkathings as well." Rhaeve commanded strongly, but with kindness in her voice.

Bhola had trouble convincing Feena that it was safe to leave the cave. Feebra rushed out into the sun, spotting Rhaeve, he rushed to her, and hugged her without knowing why. The timid milkathings came to her shyly, and rubbed their velvet noses against her in affection. Even untrusting Feena came forward and dropped to her knees and hugged The Rhaeve. The Rhaeve placed her golden hand upon the head of Feena, and Feena stopped shuddering--- a quick glow went over Feena and was gone instantly.

Bhola had never seen Feena ever embrace another living creature. Bhola himself had never been touched by Feena. Even Feebra was only touched in anger. Strange things were afoot, but somehow Bhola knew they were for the good of his life.

Feena made a covering for Rhaeve's budding womanhood, and the small party left the cave.

"Why do the large ones call the homeland of the Nod the badlands?" Bhola asked Rhaeve.

"I suppose it's because it's a harsh place for them."

"But it not a bad land. It only hard on those that not learn the ways," Feena put in.

"Yes I suppose it would have been better named--the Hardland." Rhaeve agreed, not really interested in the conversation, as her interest was occupied by a small group of White

Riders hidden by a small pile of stones. Rhaeve knew their intentions.

"Can you know who they are?" Bhola asked in awe.

"Yes I know of their presence," Rhaeve smiled.

"Truly you are her of the sight without sight, the hearing without hearing, and the Great Sight."

"How can you know they are ahead?" Rhaeve asked Bhola.

"Because it is the way of those of Nod," Bhola replied.

"And that is my answer. It is also for those of my kind to know that which is not apparent to others," Rhaeve said.

"What do we call you Great one?" Feena asked quietly.

"You and all of your tribe to come may call me--Friend, for you have wakened me from the sleep of the dead. And for that I am ever in your debt. I am your friend for that good will you bear me in your hearts, I am your Rhaeve." Rhaeve said stopping. "Come now walk in a circle around me and fear not that which you will see. It will not harm you" Rhaeve told them with feeling.

As the mounted riders came into sight, a sudden glowing circled Rhaeve and her small band. The horses halted without command from their riders. The spears dipped in respect, and the small band of warriors sat in silence as the circle of light passed. Hours later when the light had passed, the Riders regained their ability to move.

"What has gone by?" they asked of each other.

"It is a God of the North, and we must follow the god, but we are to follow from a distance. I Stormrider of the clan of Storm Haven decide. . . Do others decide otherwise?"

None challenged their war-chief. Stormrider had proven his quick anger in the past, and in spite of his temper, he was considered to be fair in judgment and action.

"Why do we follow?" asked a young warrior, his youth marked by his hair being bound in a single braid.

"Because it is our destiny to be the guard of the light. My father before me traveled the badlands in search of the light. And his father before him. We have been blessed to be chosen by the gods. That is why! Consider that you will have songs sung about you, and you only a single-braid. Strange are the ways of gods. But strange or no, they are for us to obey, and never to challenge, so it is sung." Stormrider told the youth. And so the armed war-party followed from a distance, as it was foreseen by the hated Dervisals, and sung by the Westernesters. And now it was being fulfilled. A song fulfilled was great honor to the warriors that were fortunate enough to become part of a song.

The light went out ahead and the

war-party followed at a distance, but close enough to assist and protect from the rear.

The Song was of a young untried Girl-God, and she must be followed until she came to the place of the Calling, that was soon to be. The Witch of the Westernest had seen many happenings, great, and long to be sung of. In the lifetime of every Trueman-- a Calling was proclaimed through all the land of Nod, even into the ice of the Riders, and even into the land of the Dervisals.

Stomrider's little band of spearmen was excited by the prospect of becoming part of a great song, for songs were never forgotten and the life of man was as a twitch of an eye.

"If we are to guard the young god, why do we not ride with her, to protect her better?" asked a single braid.

"We would only frighten the small Nodites that are with her. She has forbidden us coming closer, until she wishes it," the great triple-manned Stormrider, scowled at the single-manned son of Thurt. "One time Thurtson, you'll ask of me one question too many. And that question

I will answer with spear!" Stormrider growled.

Thurtson looked away, and the band continued in silence.

Dark came slowly, bringing extreme cold. Bhola found a small hollow in the sand, out of the wind, and set about building a snug fire. The Nodites ate a handful of nutritious dried insects, and watered the milkathings. For the White Riders of the North, it was not so easy, they had no food for horse or themselves, and the little water they had went to their great horses.

"We will not last another day without water, Stormrider," a grizzled rider of four braids said, respectfully, but with worry in his old voice.

"Aye good Fulfson, we be needing water the morrow."

"Though we can't approach the young god, we can all think hard of our need. Should I tell the men?"

"Aye, tell the men. If the god not help…we are lost, good and true friend," Stormrider muttered, deep in thought.

The horses were ringed in a tight circle, for warmth and defense the men slept lightly between their trusty mounts, the horses complained through the night in thirst and hunger, and their complaints were answered by the melodious crooning of the two milkathings.

Early in the morning as they were breaking camp, the Nodites had milked the animals and were getting ready for travel.

"We must help the riders or they will die this day," Rhaeve told Bhola, her voice worried.

"They are our enemy, and the Nod takes that which belongs not in the Nod. It is the way...It has always been the way."

"Ways can be changed," Rhaeve replied softly.

"I am afraid of the changing of the ways". Bhola replied.

"Yes, I see you are afraid. But then I see you are afraid of all that you understand not! And you understand only the ways of surviving in the Nod. I think it is time for you to take a step forward in the name of your people." Rhaeve stated.

"But they are enemy!" persisted Bhola.

"Only hate and ignorance is enemy-- small one!"

"I will find water... If any exists," Bhola said. Upset that the Golden One was angry with him.

"I am only a child of Nod... Be not angry with me Princess. Your ways are the ways of the Gods themselves. I am only a poor creature of the Nod. Forgive me my ignorance. I have long hated, the riders, as all my people before me, but I will find water if water be here," Bhola blurted, his boy-man voice close to breaking.

"I impose strange requests on you my little friend, and things alien to you, worry not, for you will do what is right and you will be stronger and more a man for the doing."

And the journey continued into the morning without water being found by Bhola. By high noon, Rhaeve could feel the agony of the great horses that followed less than a mile behind.

"Is there no water to be found?" Rhaeve asked Bhola.

"No, there is none short of Fishfind." replied Bhola.

"The great horses will never reach Fishfind, I feel death is at their throats even as we speak. I am going to them now, I want you to set up camp, and under no circumstances look back. Do not even let the milkathings look where I am. Bind their eyes, then bind your own eyes... If you disobey, you will be without sight forever... That will be your penalty for not obeying. Do you understand?" Rhaeve spoke quietly, watching them closely.

"Yes! Yes!" they replied frightened. Feebra was wide eyed.

As Rhaeve approached the White Riders, the great war horses neighed softly in welcome.

The Riders were each at the head of his mount, talking gently and trying to convince the great beasts to move forward.

"Force not the noble beasts." Rhaeve commanded, breaking into their line of vision from behind a dune of glittering sand.

"They can move nowhere without water. You are the band leader?" Rhaeve stated, asking a question, that both she and the person spoken to knew was not a question, but a statement of fact.

"Yes I am Stormrider, First War-Chief to Stoneson-the-Fierce himself. And I can see that you are the Rhaeve of Rha. You are the Great Bringer of ways new to Rhapour... You have been sung of by fireside by warriors of StormHaven--since song be sung of old," Stormrider said, dropping to both knees, but with body held proudly straight. All the outriders of Storm Haven followed their chief's example.

"Never in our songs did we sing of your great beauty, only of your power and greatness in bringing better ways for man to follow," Stormrider said. He was dumfounded that she had hair of hammered silver and ice, practically to the ground, unbound and shimmering with a thousand lights. Her great eyes closed in peace. All songs sung of the Great One that walked with surety of way. And without ever opening an eye to see the way. Some songs sung of her blindness, yet having great sight without seeing. Many songs bespoke of many strange ways, but none sung of her youth, of her smallness, and of her radiant beauty.

Although a marry-man, Stormrider felt that before the day was longer, the younger Riders of the Search would follow this enchanting, diminutive child into the gates of

Derva itself. Gladly would they ride to a certain death. Stormrider knew that he too would ride into the hole of death itself, if only this child wished it for him. Not for the same reasons as the younger riders, but with great unexplained love, as a father for a wondrous child. Stormrider knew the search of Storm Haven was over, and he also knew great tasks were at hand.

"Are you all so sure of who I be?" Rhaeve said, smiling at the inner thoughts of confusion she read in the young riders.

"Who else could cause a glowing in the night? Who else could approach our great war steeds?" Stormrider asked. "These great beasts of war permit no person to enter our presence without our greeting...They greeted you at a distance without our leave. No, I know that you are the One that is sung of."

Rhaeve approached Stormrider. Rhaeve's small, slim hand placed on the head of the great war beast settled it down on all fours. Its brown liquid eyes closed, and it was immediately asleep. "Bring all the great beasts in a circle around me that I may protect them from what is to come," Rhaeve ordered kindly, in musical voice that thrilled all that heard.

"Princess Rhaeve, the beasts need water, not sleep."

"They will have water, and so will you, but first there are things to do before the water will come."

"There is no cloud. From where will rain come to this terrible land of heat and death?" Stormrider asked.

"Do not question my ways. Just bring the great beasts in a line, so that I may do what I can to save them, and you too doubting Stormrider. From this day forward you shall be known as Stormrider the Doubter. I The Rhaeve of Rha, decree this to be."

All riders looked to their Chief to see his reaction of being spoken to so severely. Never had even Stoneson the First Rider of all Storm Haven ever spoke to proud and valorous Stormrider in such a way. They all knew it would be banishment for a woman of the Haven to speak to as great a rider as Stormrider in such a disrespectful manor. And for another rider to challenge him so strongly would have meant a fight to the death...But Stormrider only laughed a great happy laugh, as he got to his feet to execute the order given.

Each rider stood at the head of his mount, and as Rhaeve walked along the line of kneeling horses, she placed her hand upon the head of each great beast, causing each horse to fall over in sleep.

"Do you require the touch of sleep, or can you be trusted to keep your eyes closed and your backs to me?" Rhaeve asked the gathering of awe-struck warriors.

"What say you?" Stormrider addressed his men-at-arms.

To a man, they agreed to control their own destiny without the help of being touched into sleep. Although they trusted Rhaeve, they all looked to their sleeping horses with fear.

"I see fear, but not mistrust of me, only doubt of the unknown. That is normal for warriors that intend on surviving the trials of warfare, but it is a misplaced fear that you will soon have no longer." Rhaeve told the small gathering of warriors.

"What are you about?" Stormrider asked, not as a challenge, only as a chief seeking direction.

"Go to the heads of your beasts and kneel facing north as the beasts are, under no circumstances turn and look, for it will bring blindness or death. Wrap your heads and close your eyes tightly. Hurry! I will go for the water."

Rhaeve quickly walked to an outcropping of granite, less than five hundred steps away. The sky was clear and blue, not a cloud to the horizon.

Great rumbling filled the sky, and the men kept their heads down, the

Nodites to the south lay flat in abject fear, holding the heads of their terrified milkathings. Shortly Rhaeve was beside the Nodites.

"You can take the coverings from your eyes, and from the eyes of your beasts as well." Rhaeve told the terrified Nodites.

"Are we alive, or have we crossed over to the other-world of our fathers?" Bhola asked, looking around to see if the setting was familiar.

"You are alive," Rhaeve laughed.

"Is there water?" Bhola asked, looking to the sky for rain bearing clouds. The sky was cloudless.

"How can there be water without rain?" Feena asked.

"Come," Rhaeve replied, walking towards the outcropping.

As they approached the granite outcropping, a gurgling and falling of water could be heard by the frantic milkathings, who ran ahead and drank greedily from the bubbling spring that dribbled water through a small burned-black hole on the edge of a natural dish of white granite. The water ran clear and was slowly filling the natural depression in the stone. It was a small depression, less than three feet in depth and about ten across.

The Nodites dragged the milkathings away, before they bloated with too much water. Feena started to fill their water skins for the trip ahead.

"No need for that Feena." Rhaeve said.

"No need to carry water?" Feena asked, clearly not understanding the meaning of Rhaeve.

"No. This is to be the place of peace in Nod. Where all can come to water. This place shall be known as Bhola's Pool. For a great garden shall grow here for you. And all that travel through the badlands of Nod shall know that this is a place of refuge. Bhola and Feena shall be the parents of the greatest tribe of Nod. Richness and goodness shall surely be your reward for wakening the Rhaeve. I command you now: You shall turn none away--thirsty nor hungry, even though their purse be empty, and they be even of the Dervisal. All Rhapour shall benefit from this endless spring that came of its own accord from the bowels of the earth. However, caravans that can afford to pay, shall pay as is fair in this desolate place."

"And how shall we protect it from those that would raid and drive us away?" Feena asked."

"The way will not be a way of war but an Oasis of Refuge, that all will benefit from. A place of peace that will welcome all that travel these hostile lands."

"Those are noble thoughts Rhaeve ... Noble indeed, but when you leave, who will enforce the peace?" Feena asked.

"Hush! The Riders approach." Rhaeve commanded.

"Permission is humbly requested to approach the Pool of Bhola, the Keeper of the Garden." Stormrider asked.

"Permission granted," Bhola said without realizing he had replied so bravely and naturally to the great bearded warrior that faced him.

"Strange happenings are afoot," Stormrider told his riders who were in a single line behind their war leader. As each great shaggy warrior approached the pool they asked Bhola's permission to approach the pool. Somehow they knew that they could not approach the pool without the consent of the Keeper of the Pool. And somehow Bhola knew that if he refused that they could not physically attack him or take water by force.

After filling their water-bags and returning to their mounts with the precious life-giving water, the warriors sat with their horses, and were in awe of that which controlled them without their knowing the why of. "We here are part of a great beginning that is only an awakening of great powers. The Rhaeve is not the child as she appears," Fulfson the elder, counseled his chief.

"Yes, it is a great power that can bring the water of life through the rock of Nod. And it is a stranger power that can put thoughts and words to a warriors lip," agreed Stormrider

"We are blessed to be in this Riding, and in winters too far in the coming to count. . . We here shall be spoken of with great respect. Such is our fate for Riding with this One... As a child she appears, yet only a god could wield such power."

After watering their horses the Riders gently coaxed their war beasts to follow them to the Pool. When they arrived, they again found themselves asking for permission to approach the Pool, and they knew to a man that it would be impossible to draw their axes or draw a dagger in anger. The person of Rhaeve was strong upon the place, and all felt it deeply.

Soon the horses were well watered and water skins filled.

"Bhola... In this rock I will reside forever, and between us there is the bond of your awakening the power that is in me. This power will live in this place with you and your tribe forever. Fear nothing, and harm nothing, for your covenant with me is one of peace. To break it will dry the Pool and I will reside in this place no longer. Remember that your great strength is in peace. Keep this one covenant and your tribe will endure forever in this place in greatness. Break it and you will be less than a grain of sand underfoot."

The granite stone beneath their feet rumbled, as if agreeing to this covenant between Bhola of Nod and The Rhaeve. And so the small party of warriors left with Rhaeve upon the back of a pony birthed in the badlands by a war horse. This pony would know no other rider.

With her small party Rhaeve returned to Fishfind.

FISHFIND

The heavily armed war party swooped into Fishfind in search of water for their great steeds. The peaceful inhabitants long being aware of the approaching war party had taken to the ocean in their great canoes in fear of being murdered by these strange white savages from the north. Only the empty village and Thum and his mighty sons were left to greet the White Warriors.

"Ho…."Challenged Thumson, "Why have you come to our village bearing arms? Do you come in peace?" Thumson asked holding the great ax of his father.

"And who can you be? You appear as sons of the Northern Keep, yet I see no horses." Stormrider asked, not as a challenge, and with his war lance held high in non-aggression.

"He be my son. That's who he be. But who do you be? More zactly-- Why be you here a Fishfind? You be far from the Keep. In these troubling times a true Rider a the Keep should be tending to tha business a tha Keep, not bothering them that be mindin thar own affairs. Far you be from home," Thum replied with quiet authority.

"And who be you?" challenged Stormrider. "You have the look about you of a Rider. Yet we see no horse nor sign of the mighty friends to us Warders of the Keep," Stormrider stated, all the time moving his great steed around the small group of blond giants that were even greater in stature than his own hand-picked group of outriders.

"My name be Thum. And I be from as old a family as yar be. Whatear yar family. Though I be old--talk not down to me wahout respect, nor look to me wahout respect. For all my year's I'll haul yar from tha noble beast yar sit so prettily hupon, ahaps your thought of self will not be large as it be now."

Fulfson of the four-braids answered, "We come in peace. And the First Rider surely means no lack of respect. Thum you say your name be... In my youth there be stories of a mighty warrior of the Keep who tired of war, took his father's great ax in hand and left the Keep. Some say he lived in the Shadow Forest...Some of the elders claimed that he and Thurma the dotter to Thurma-the-Just left on foot, and lived in the Shadow Forest itself ... But the Old Ones in their dotage are given to imagination, specially on cold nights at fireside when the jug helps to warm the body and warm the imagination as well. Sometime the imagination it be well given to create that which we wants, payin no heed to fact. What say you?"

"I not want to argue wa a four braided warrior. But I be sayin that I be tha same Thum a left tha Keep mor'n a hundred' n twenty winter gone by. And tha ax born by my oldest be tha same as in tha stories of old," Thum challenged.

"Not callin yar a bloney teller. Just tellin that tales of fireside be carried far and not always true," Fulfson concluded.

"Why is my noblest of friends being questioned? I have the answer to the riddle. Do any challenge me?" Rhaeve asked, with humor in her voice.

"Be it my Rhaeve? My child from the sea" ... Thurma exploded from behind her towering sons.

Rhaeve burst from behind her ring of warriors and the child and old woman embraced, both laughing and crying and hugging.

"How can you still be alive Thurma-mother? Your life allotment is a hundred winters at the most. You must be a hundred and seventy, if you are a day. How is it possible?"

"It be the pond by the tree. When you left, Thum hisself cut the tree as you commanded. The Great Beastie left for the deep, and Thum built us a home of the wood of the tree. We have lived in the house for a hundred years. Never gettin much older."

"Have you been drinking the water of the pond?" Rhaeve asked the old woman.

"We be drinkin of the water since before the first born arrived." Thurma said, holding Rhaeve at arms length and looking deep into the liquid gold eyes of the Princess. "We be doin wrong?" Thurma asked looking deep into the liquid gold for an answer not spoken aloud.

Rhaeve laughed.

"No. No. You have done no harm. And by the looks of these wondrous giants you have born, I'd say you have done great good by drinking of the pond water. But tell me--has Thragg never returned in all these years?"

"Aye the great beast comes ever month and spends a day swimmin in the pond. He talks to no one save my oldest. And what they talk of is secret to me. Not that I cares what Thumson and the great frightenin thing have to talk of."

"If you care to know of what I talk of with the great person, you may ask me direct, and I shall answer as direct as I can," Thumson put in without being addressed by either his mother or the princess.

"Careful of respect........ Woodschopper," Thurtson challenged.

"Meant no disrespect. . . Single--braid! Just sayin truth. Nothin wrong in sayin truth! You have trouble with truth?" Thumson asked coyly. The two young men measured each other carefully.

While the Outriders busied themselves with the caring for their great horses and the sons of Thum called in the canoes, Rhaeve and Thurma talked quietly together. All the time Thum butting in and hugging Rhaeve.

"Never had no girl-child. The big fool still thinks of you as our little girl. And you are still a girl-child... Even if we know that you are over a hundred winters," Thurma told Rhaeve.

"My winters as you say are at least a hundred that you know of ...." Rhaeve said to Thurma, while wondering to herself if her winters could be counted. She knew that she had no idea of her real age. She knew that for all the world to see she was just a little girl barely into puberty. Yet she knew that she was older than could be calculated by these simple folk.

After the return of the gentle Fishfinders, and the general feasting by all, Rhaeve and Thumson sat face to face for hours.

"They be still huddled at another?" Thum asked.

"Hush now you old fussy. You know that Rhaeve's ways are not our ways. And she not be going to hurt your baby boy."

"Hrrrrrrmpphhh!" was Thum's reply, and shortly his great ax could be heard angrily creating a woodpile.

By early dawn Rhaeve had a great deal of information about Thragg, his purpose, the fate of the Rhanian princes, and other vague information about herself, the Old Ones, the Great Mother and even a very hazy imprint about bothersome serpents. Whatever they were. For Rhaeve it was a highly informative night. Thumson on the other hand was feeling thoughts that were not becoming of a brother, and especially a brother of such an obviously child-like sister.

Rhaeve knew that she must wait until the next coming of the orca. She spent days mind-calling him, but to no avail. Either her calling power was too weak... Or the New found king of the deep wasn't interested in being called to the hateful land where he had suffered for thousands of years. In any case: Thragg came not to Fishflnd.

Soon he will come, Rhaeve thought to herself, for she knew that without his monthly return to the pond his years would soon be ones that could be counted. Even a Rhapourian with fleeting existence could mark the years of the Orca. Rhaeve knew Thragg would soon come.

THE GARDEN

"Will you come up where I can see you?" The serpent peevishly inquired of the Old One who was sleeping deep in the effervescence of the well. The Old One pretended to be sleeping too deeply to hear. And the feathered serpent knew this. The serpent found small rocks and dropped them into the well to aggravate the Old One. The Old One chuckled silently and built a resistance into the bubbling fluid that caused the fluid to reject anything falling into it. And the Old One caused it to happen with considerable force.

"Well I know now for certain that you're awake. And I don't find you a bit clever. I think you are a nasty old meany, just taking advantage of a poor helpless girl. And a girl that you have sworn on the Ultimate Oath of the KEEPERS to obey forever. You are down there awake. And I know it.

COME UP!" screamed the multi-colored Serpent peering over the ledge suspiciously, and careful of some new trick by her guardian.

"How can you abandon me? You are sworn to obedience and servitude as a Supreme Guardian to the Universe. I am my Mother's daughter; and that makes me the prime citizen of the whole wide universe... And you know it. So come up."

Deep in the peaceful bubbling of life-dreams the Old One opened one blind eye in malevolence. Then sent up a small charge of anger to scare the pretty little pest away. The Old One knew she was in no danger. He knew she was just interested in sitting and talking in his face. Aha! That gave the Old One an idea .He opened his other blind eye and peered up to see if the pest was still peeking over the edge. He couldn't see her with his blind vision, so he projected the surface picture down into his mind's eye.

Just as he suspected, there she was preening her feathers, and very safe in an ahpoo tree.

The Old One knew that she had been eating that damn fruit of thought-provoking again. She knew it was forbidden to all but the Old Ones in the universe; but like her great mother, she too had acquired a taste for the forbidden fruit. And because of his inability to tamper with the thought patterns the Old One was restricted to trickery and bribery to keep the young pest away from his One Tree... This was his tree, and no other than he could eat from it. It was the law of all universes. The One Tree was a bearer of forbidden fruit. Except to the Old One in his many forms. His other three forms had let their trees die, and now they were sleeping the deep sleep, waiting for him to rejoin himself and continue with the raising of four new trees, and planning new futures and existences. But right now the pest was busy daintily peeling an ahpoo, and her thoughts directed at him were a challenge to stop her. Well he wasn't rising for one little ahpoo. What was another little ahpoo going to mean after the amount she had already consumed. He shut blind eyes.

"I know you are awake. If you ignore me I will eat this Ahpoo," she challenged, provocatively licking the ahpoo with her little red tongue.

"Who cares," he thought to himself, drifting off to sleep.

"You had better care. Or are you afraid to care? Maybe you are afraid to care--after the tamperiiiiiing!" she screamed down at him. Then she undantily gulped the whole ahpoo down in one swallow.

The water changed from a cool bubbling to a rapid boiling, with a strange aroma of sulfur and other nauseous smells. She knew that he was now fully awake and very angry with her, for to call a Guardian a tamperer was the ultimate insult ...Especially if it was true.

The Guardian emerged from the well with a sputtering and a hissing of the well's opening. Drops of thick yellow fluid ran down the Old One's robe, burning the ground raw and black wherever it fell.

"Thought you were sleeping."

"Sleeping. Sleeeeping. I'll give you Sleeeeeeping." The Old One roared up at the tree.

The serpent flew to a higher branch, and broadcast her widest band of loving with her tightest control. He wilted as she knew he would. She was getting more control all the time. Even the miserable Old One admitted this.

"Can we leave this place soon?" She asked, before he regained complete control of his being. She knew that each time he returned from wherever he went in the well it took longer for him to get in control of himself, and to attune himself to the environment, that he was not to tamper with.

"Well.... You have my attention," he remarked icily.

"Your undivided attention," she replied suspiciously.

"Yes," he replied, already bored with her company.

"How do I know that you are not just one of those images you used to trick me with... How do I know that you are not still down there doing whatever it is you do in that stupid well... Is it really a well? Or is that also just another of your stupid tricks? I'm going to tell mother everything when I see her."

"If you ever see her." replied the Old One menacingly.

"What's that supposed to mean? Now you are threatening me again. Seems the only time you're not threatening me is when you're ignoring me. What do you say to that?"

Silence from the Old One.

The young serpent flew down and landed on the Old One's shoulder. "Just checking," she told him daintily in his ear. "Just making sure that you hadn't gone and left a specter to talk to me."

"You are such an untrusting girl. If you can't learn to trust me, who will you ever be able to trust?" The Old One asked.

"No one!" she laughed gleefully, flapping her beautiful wings together in joy. She could tell by the way the Old One scowled that he was happy that she had passed his little test. She had long since known that the Old One never said anything without it being some kind of training or testing or evaluating or some other dumb thing that he would not tell her about. Well she decided two could play that stupid game. And seldom she gave him any idea that she knew he was always working with her. She pretended that they were just talking. But she knew otherwise.

"While you've been sleeping in that stupid well, I've been busy planting ahpoo trees." Circe told the Old One coyly.

"You have grown since last we talked." The Old One said. Completely ignoring the attempt by Circe to get him away from the well. "You are becoming more like your mother every day. Yes you will grow into a very beautiful lady if you quit telling lies."

"I just thought it would be nice if we walked around the Garden together. I have been to the edge, but the natives would kill me if they could enter the Garden…Why can they not enter the garden?" Circe asked.

"Because it's your garden. And they can't enter it without asking your permission."

"How could they do that? We don't understand each other, and if I gave them permission to enter, they would try and kill me. So they can stay where they are."

"And there lies the problem," replied the Old One.

"What is the problem?" asked Circe seriously.

"Always the problem is the same. Each thinking being wants and demands justice and rights... For themselves when it is not forthcoming they howl INJUSTICE! Yet, they in turn are not very good about allowing others with a different viewpoint or lifestyle to have their rights. And while they deprive others of rights they wail how unfair life is to them. If we ever solve this small problem all other large problems will be no more."

"If this is the prime problem in the universe of living creatures and you know it. Tell my mother and she can stop all things living from thinking in this dreadful manner. Then I can leave this garden," Circe laughed, all the time skipping prettily around the Old One.

"Were it that simple," the old One answered tiredly.

"Well if it is the problem. Just order it to stop."

"Then I would not be stopping it. All I would be doing is imposing my idea of freedom and rights upon others. And that is already the problem. Each entity must work its way up the ladder of evolution on its own merits-- Otherwise they would not be fulfilling their destiny. Your mother has great power Circe. She has powers to destroy galaxies. She has the power to annihilate all living organisms including thinking creatures. She could turn this planet in to a ball of cinder in an instant. But she cannot have all living creatures thinking identical thoughts. If they did, they would lose their special identities that make all living things unique and different. As long as they have control of their inner self, they can only be shepherded to a better way. In the past she has shown less understanding and in her wrath has caused whole cultures, even planets to be no more. In her maturity and wisdom she interferes less and tries indirect guidance. And that leaves us with our problem unsolved."

"This is terribly confusing and it gives me a headache. I don't want to understand it. I just want to leave this garden."

"Yes I know of wants, and needs, and rights, and what is fair and unfair in the universe. And it is what it is, and what it is gives me a pain in the. . ." The Old One's thoughts drifted off, and he walked away leaving the youngster in mental anguish.

At least she is thinking and planning again. Were she not so lazy and self serving, things could be different. Ah well, enough pain and maybe she will find a way to solve the problem, the Old One mused, drifting into his swirling well.

Circe flew to the top of an ahpoo tree and devoured all the bright red fruit in sight, making herself very sick.

Happy thoughts ran through the Old One's head as he watched the troubled child eating fruit of her own free will, fruit that he could never force her to eat. It was so vile in taste that Circe would never dream of eating it if not for its being forbidden to her... Maybe with enough anger and fruit she could become great enough to solve the problem for all eternity...And maybe not. But the old Keeper of the garden could only wait and watch. As had forever been the way.

Circe was the first of her kind to eat of the fruit.

Maybe she would affect other changes.

And then there was the first awakening of a Rhaeve.

Possibilities.... Possibilities...... Possibilities....

ORCA

Rhaeve called the mighty Orca from the sea. And he came with great reluctance.

"Why have you resisted answering my call?"

"I would tell you a lie gentle princess, but I see that I cannot do this. Yes I have heard your calls. Fault not a poor beast for choosing freedom to be with his mate and child over the endless loneliness of a small stagnant pond."

"I seek only information great one. Why do you think that I would force you to return to such a miserable way of life?"

"It is not for me to know the ways of those that command great power. It is only my destiny to answer it, and to obey. If I am to return to the pond, then I will do so, but not with joy. If you wish that I return to that pond--

command me, and if I must return I will, but with a sad heart in leaving my family."

"If whoever you have so honorably served for untold years has had no consideration for you. This I can do nothing about, but I can treat you as I would wish to be treated. And I would not wish to be treated to an eternity in a slimy old pond....Whatever the great plan. No plan can be so important as to leave a living sensitive creature in such a place with no thought for the well-being of the creature. Sometimes I wonder at the greatness of the Great Ones."

"But with your power you too must be a Great One."

"No, whatever I am: I am not of the ilk that could leave you at that pond for thousands of years. And that brings us to the reason for calling you," Rhaeve said.

"And that is?"

"I have been sleeping since we last met, and if you are concerned about being sent to a pond, I am as deeply concerned about being put into limbo."

"Limbo... Again?"

"Since last we met. All but for a few days of travel I have been sleeping again. And I assure you not by choice."

"How could you... You of such power be put to sleep without your wanting it to happen," Thragg asked wonder in his voice.

"It seems that if I get away from light for a short period of time I simply go to sleep."

"This is indeed strange, but at the worst, it can only be aggravating." speculated the great orca.

"It's more than aggravating to be physically 12 winters old by this planet's time, and possibly hundreds of thousands of light years by real time, and not even have any awareness of the meager 12 winters."

"As I see it, you can do nothing about that which has happened in the past, but you can insure that it will not take place in the future."

"Yes I suppose, now that I know the cause of my 'sleeping sickness' it will take little in the way of precaution to ensure it not happening again. And this is why I have come to you. I know you to be an honorable friend. I wish to make an arrangement with you to mind contact with me on every full moon."

"And if I can't make contact?"

"Then come and find me, for I am in trouble and helpless to do anything about it. And on the other hand, if I hear nothing from you, then I will come to your aid."

"You are suggesting a pact of mutual dependency and protection? You a Rhanian would make a covenant with a mere Orca?" Thragg asked.

"Mere Orca!" Rhaeve exclaimed in anger.

"There are no MERE anythings in my minds eye. . . All things great and small, whether they walk or crawl, have importance to me, and any power that finds it otherwise will have me to contend with, for I see this is my destiny. It has been yours to wait for me. Well that was unfair, but I intend to make your vigil not one that was totally worthless. I intend to honor it with some meaning. I don't intend to let all these years in a pond be for nothing!"

Thragg looked down on the small helpless-looking child, and was glad that she was not angry with him.

"Peers as the weak and the meek, just got a monster to champion their cause," Thragg grinned.

"I'll meek and weak you." Rhaeve laughed, up at the giant.

Far out to sea the pod called to their leader, and Thragg knew that they had a friend who cared. A small powerful one.

"You must mind link and tell me all you know of this planet and yourself, where you come from... You must tell me everything. I know so little, yet I see that I have much to do, and it will be easier if I have some knowledge."

Such a small creature to have such a great heart, thought Thragg to himself. "Never worry about having a friend to call, as long as you are within distance of orca, for from this day forward all orcas shall heed the call of Rhaeve and her tribe. In water you shall be forever as safe as an orca can make your journey through our land of water," Thragg promised, thinking to himself that this small creature would undoubtedly find friends on land, in air, and even in deep space itself ... But what was deep-space? Thragg wondered to himself.

And so they mind linked deep into the night.

Rhaeve learned much that made no sense, but she could clearly see that with his great mental capacity, Thragg had been invaluable in charting and navigating through the galaxies. But she could see that was all in the past. Something had destroyed his ability to recall accurately, and those he had navigated for had become hopelessly stranded on this outlying planet. Without his ability they would never leave this planet.

Rhaeve could see that they were alive, though not well, they were alive, and waiting... waiting for what?

In the morning, Rhaeve had a clear picture of seeking out Marples the Great. Deep in Thragg's mind was a vague picture of information known by Marples, Many answers that Rhaeve needed.

Thragg could only wonder why such a great task had been set out for such a small physically helpless creature. One that could not even stay awake! Without memory. And with no idea of her latent powers.

"At least she has no wrong ideas of the universe, and the way things should be. Maybe that is her strength, not her weakness," Thragg told his mate as his pod mind-locked. Thragg could see that his pod-mates felt sorrow for the small child that was saddled with such an enormous task.

Thragg and his pod mind-locked with all the other wild pods in the deep and made a pact to forever be friend to the tribe that bore the mark of Rha. And in the recesses of the complex being known as Rhaeve there was always a special place for the children of the deep. Ever would the progeny of Thragg, and the true followers of Rhaeve have a bonding.

A FAITHFUL VANGUARD

As Rhaeve sat at the pool and mind-linked by the hour without a word or sign of life showing from either her or the orca, The White Riders, and the Sons of Thum fidgeted in the background.

"Narent right. Taint normal." Thumson said, aloud, to no one in particular.

"Agreed," Stormrider replied, showing his teeth in friendship.

This was the first sign of anything other than pure hostility and an obvious desire to try lance against ax.

Soon the two leaders were deep in talk. Wine flowed freely and both armed camps found common cause. They all had an overpowering compulsion to protect and champion the small child. Before the sun had risen, the sons of Thum and the

White Rider's had sworn to a brotherhood of allegiance to the Princess Rhaeve.

"Then all agree?" Thumson said, looking to his brothers and the White Riders for conformation.

"Agreed... Agreed... Agreed..." Came the reply from every voice. And it came with strong feeling in each voice.

"Then we'll seal it with a blood grasp of brotherhood!" Thumson declared, sinking his great double bladed razor sharp ax into a stump. He placed his palm on the blade, then held his bleeding palm out to be shaken in the deep blood-grasp of the Northern White Riders.

Each man solemnly approached the ax and soon each man had soundly and seriously grasped the bleeding hand of every man present.

Women and children were excluded from the blood-grasping, as it was a serious man-affair, and not to be tainted with the inexperience of youth, nor the softness of female presence.

No drink nor food was taken that day, and the women and children stayed clear of the man-happening. Secretly the women considered it to be foolish, and the boys bragged quietly to girls of the blood grasping they would do when they were men.

The following day the sons of Thum busied themselves with the sharpening of their great axes. The White Riders also busied themselves with their gear of war. For all swore to guard the Rhaeve with their lives, and to never abandon her until her Great Quest was done. None felt good about starting the journey by facing the Gorge of Death, but none let his new-found Brother of Blood know of such woman-like fears.

"Why'nt take tha Thragg?" old Thum asked.

"His time is not now," Rhaeve replied, simply.

"He would be a greater warrior in tha Gorge than Sons to me An' tha white horsers," Thum continued.

"Do you make light of our courage old man?" Thurtson challenged.

"Mind your manners!" Fulfson roared.

"I don't need old men telling me my manners" Thurtson said angrily.

"Perhaps I could tell you your place," Stormrider said, quickly getting to his feet. "We are guests of these good folk, and what of your brotherhood rites just taken. Were they of no meaning? You are of single braid, and Fulfson is of four. This alone is reason for respect to Fulfson. And if reason and good manners are not cause for courtesy--There are other ways of teaching courtesy."

The rest of the White Riders shook their shaggy heads in agreement with their war-chief. Thurtson sat down and glared. The dark looks were returned with equal fervor from every Son of Thum.

"Meant no disrespect to tha or tha others," Thum said to Stormrider. "Only meant tha a monster such as Thragg'd have better chance a facing terrible beasties a be 'bout the Gorge. No warriors ever come back a tha horrid place. By the past, many go, none ta home come."

"I know this. And so do my men. Only Thurtson's youthful foolish pride makes him a thorn," Stormrider told Thum.

"Pride can have advantages... None of you were even thinking of the protection of Fishfind in your fervor to protect me. If not for this over sensitive youth, you bearers of arms would have left the village unprotected," Rhaeve said.

"True," agreed both Thumson and Stormrider.

"You will stay and form a guard to protect the village until we return," Stormrider told Thurtson.

"And I have no say in this?" Thurtson blurted.

"None," answered Stormrider firmly. "Do you challenge my decision Thurtson?" he continued softly.

"No, I will stay and do as you order. I will stay until you return, and do as you would expect of me. I apologize to all present for my remarks. I thought a slur was meant, and I would be no son to my father, nor would I deserve to ride with this good company if I sat still while I thought we were insulted. I made a mistake in judgment. Sometimes I am too quick to take action."

All agreed that Thurtson had acted out of youth, but with courage, if not thought.

"It would be wise to seek counsel from Thum in our absence."

"I will listen to Thum in all things, but if the village needs defense, I will take charge," Thurston replied.

"To my thinking, the younger be fine." Thum said.

In all the conversation, Rhaeve had not said a word, she only smiled inwardly.

Soon the guard was ready to travel.

"We see you again child?" Thrum said, holding her two small hands in his old paw. Thurma had both arms around Rhaeve and tears were running freely down her wrinkled cheeks.

"Who can say," answered Rhaeve. But Thum could see in her eyes that Rhaeve's destiny was quickly starting to unfold, and Thurma was as long in tooth as he was himself. No, they would never see this child again. A child that they loved as much as they loved their twelve sons, who they would never have been blessed with if not for Rhaeve coming into their barren lives.

"Always be close to yar," Thum said, tears forming in the corners of his proud gray eyes.

"We thank you for our blessing of Sons," Thurma said, holding the small frail child close.

The armed party left Fishfind with Rhaeve mounted on a pony directly surrounded by the twelve Sons of Thum and Thurma.

"I still be feelin better the girl be takin' the booger from tha briny, ugly tha he be, he be long a power, 'n terrible when angry."

"You be concerned for sons," Thurma said.

"Truth...Her that gave 'm ta us can take 'm... Shouda left younger one a home."

"She needs them not. The pony be all she need. Trust a Mother," Thurma said, holding Thums great paw to console the sad feeling she knew was gripping the tired old bear.

The vanguard of horsemen rode ahead, assuring a clear passage for the ax-bearing guard of brothers, who ringed Rhaeve with great seriousness, much to the entertainment of Rhaeve.

With no altercations whatever they reached the opening to the gorge in less than a week.

"It is growing dark. We camp until sun-up," Stormrider ordered his vanguard as they approached the very opening of the already black gorge.

The main guard of Thumson and his brothers set up camp. The White Riders patrolled, their great white chargers snorting angrily as they neared the mouth of the gorge.

Satisfied that the camp and surrounding area was free of any threats, the Riders dismounted and joined in with the gathering of faggots for the blazing fire... Rhaeve noticed that these otherwise brave warriors, who she knew would give up their lives in an instant in defense of her, were troubled deeply, now that they were facing the unknown...

Sleep came hard for all, all except Rhaeve.

At first light, not a member of the guard needed waking. It had not been a night of sound sleep for any of the party.

"The Rhaeve is gone!" cried a Son of Thum, finding her bedroll empty.

"Gone!" Came the anguished reply from stormrider.

"Who but a demon could have crept into an armed camp, with posted fire-keepers, and not a true sleeper. This will be scribed as a terrible night in the history of all Riders," Stormrider said, addressing no-one in particular. More likely he spoke to the winds that were howling through the camp, flattening tents, putting the fire out, and terrifying the normally overbold horses. "What do we do?" Stormrider asked Fulfson. Under normal circumstance in the face of adversity, Stormrider would seek no counsel, as his immediate reaction would be to attack any threat. But there was nothing to attack, only the rising wind

that was rapidly making it impossible
for travel.

Out of the mouth of the gorge a small
wailing started to build, sending fear
into the hearts of the valorous
warriors, and abject terror into the
hearts of the noble war horses.

Soon the Riders were hard pressed
to hold their steeds. Even with the
help of the powerful sons of Thum,
the war horses were gaining their feet
and thrashing around madly, further
destroying the camp.

"Cover their eyes... Cover their eyes,"
roared Stormrider.

Not a warrior heard, as each was
listening to inner voices of building
terror. Every warrior had his personal
monster and inner fear that all men
carry deep in their inner recesses.
Now these ghouls and monsters and
other overwhelming terrors were
turning stalwart warriors into
gibbering terror—stricken idiots.
Some collapsed-- totally overcome by
their own personal inner terror.
Others ran howling into the desert,

following the war horses in the same mindless panic as the beasts they chased. Stormrider and only four other warriors fiercely attacked in suicidal anger. Their great courage twisting their fears into a spring-board of attack.

Fulfson of the four braids was one of the few to turn and attack his personal monsters. His great heart overloaded with adrenalin and the palpitations racing so rapidly that the valorous old warrior was consumed by his old body being not up to his personal courage.

Fulfson went to his death, war ax striking deeply into the beasts before him. He died killing his personal beast. A good death, and one desired by all White Northmen, he died with ax in hand, facing a powerful foe. As he lay dying, his heart racing madly out of control. A great smile could have been seen, if there was a sane mind to view it, but there was not one.

THE GORGE OF DEATH

Rhaeve felt deeply the false bravado projected by her Courageous guard. She could see in each and every mind a Willingness to give up their lives in defense of her person. Yet, she could see that this facing the unknown was a terror to melt even these otherwise stalwart warriors. Strange is the heart of man, she thought to herself. So ready to face a host that will surely destroy them, yet reluctant to the point of uncontrollable terror to face a future that is not known to them. Mankind is a strange animal, she thought. She could clearly see that in spite of their great courage that not a man in the camp would be able to remain conscious in the opening of the gorge. And she could further see that actual penetration was impossible.

Rhaeve wondered what ingenious mind had so deeply plumed the inner workings of all minds, as to set a mental force block that would be effective on any mentality. Surely it could not be too evil, possibly not evil at all, as the barrier was not constructed to take life, only make it impossible to enter the valley.

The sagyr that she had previously encountered at the Tree appeared to greet her as she stepped into the mouth of the gorge.

Knowing that the terrible heads and slathering jaws were just a projection, she stepped in under the terrible jaws and sat in the seat. As soon as she was seated, she felt an euphoric sense of well being pervading her very being. Immediately the picture of a fresh flowing spring and contentment came to mind.

In the opening to the valley great unspeakable monsters had been gathering and slithering towards her. As soon as she sat in the seat, they instantly vanished. "That's cute," she thought to herself "all these terrible beasties--and not a tooth in the group."

Rhaeve did notice that were each great terrible slithering horror had been was actually a small self propelled ball that had a feathery antenna, and somehow she felt that each antenna was aimed at the front of the gorge, now that she was seated on the sagyr.

It appeared that whatever activated these small ball-like contrivances was deactivated the moment she sat in the seat. Testing her theory she jumped lightly from the sagyr. Immediately the sagyr stopped pretending to be an oasis of safety, and once more reared up as a terrible beast of unthinkable horror.

Rhaeve decided to walk through the valley, so as to better view all the neat impediments that would face a warrior and possibly to help her understand a mind that would construct this terrible-appearing barrier. Overhead great snakes slithered down slimy walls, giant fanged bats dived at her head, each barely missing contact. Great cracks opened unexpectedly before her bottomless and magnetically compelling her to fall in vertigo. Sticky webs over run with spiders – their great fangs dripping venom. She almost retched up her stomach, letting herself been gulfed by the putrid stench of horrors around her. Regaining her control, she mused at the imagination of a being clever enough develop enough believability to even entrap such as her in its false web of intrigue to.

The walls of the gorge closed in, taking away all air and crushing her in a deathly embrace. "Nice place for a claustrophobic," she thought to herself, stepping through the wall and continuing down through the actual valley.

A soft shimmering light of nothingness engulfed her, her feeling of contact with things real, ceased. Rhaeve could not feel anything, she drifted aimlessly through a fog of unreality. She could feel, smell, see, hear…. Nothing! She was losing identity quickly. She knew this must be another trick, yet as she tried to fathom it, self doubt, insecurity, a feeling of none-being was quickly overcoming her being, worse yet, it was being replaced by a total feeing of nothingness. As she swirled through an endless tunnel of shimmering smog, she could feel all contact with reality withering into nothingness. Ultimate vertigo spun her into a black hole that shriveled her mind, losing all contact with reality......

Rhaeve mind-screamed for help as she disintegrated into nothingness itself.

THE GARDEN

"She is no more!" Wailed Circe into the well.

"UP! UP! Come up!" Wailed Circe in terror. She knew that if the Rhaeve was lost to limbo so was she.

"What is the problem?" swirled a disinterested thought from very deep, and far away in the well.

"I need help! She needs help. Come and help," screamed the volatile feathered-being into the well.

"You'll wilt your lovely feathers if you carry on so," came a soft, soothing voice from far down in the well.

"Come up... Come up!" Circe demanded, with less vigor, as she was busy preening and checking her pretty feathers-- She hated wilting, droopy feathers. After all, if she had nothing pretty to sing to in the mirror of the pond, what would life be worth?

"Nothing…. That's what," Circe yelled down into the well

"Nothing…" Drifted up the voice of the Old One, getting closer to showing any interest in Circe.

"No--Nothing. Are you coming up so we can talk about it?"

"I suppose… If I must," came the vague, aggravated reply, from closer in the well.

Circe knew she had him angered… She liked that, for she knew he would come up, if only to chastise her. Well she didn't care, as long as he came to the surface.

The familiar sulfur and smoke drifted up from the well. Somehow it seemed stronger and caused her to cough and choke. This had never happened before. What it could mean she was not sure of. Could it be a good sign?

Probably not, she thought glumly.

"Things just keep getting worse," Circe challenged the Old One, who she knew was just below the surface. She knew this because the well was glowing almost like a beacon, sending a beam out into space.

"You were yelping about needing help--you appear just normal to me," said the Old One, thinking to himself that she was as normal as she could be.... considering...

"I don't need help. The Emerging One is losing shape. I am having trouble feeling her. You have great powers. You feel."

"Yes... Yes... Yes..." the Old One muttered.

"Can you feel her?"

"I can feel her just fine. She is facing a test."

"Help her before she is no more," demanded Circe.

"And what will that avail you?"

"It will keep her alive. If she ceases to be, I'll be stranded in this terrible garden forever. That's what it will avail me! Sometimes I think you see the world through a very clouded set of eyes.... Do you have eyes?"

"To answer your last question: Not the kind you would recognize as eyes. As to keeping her alive: If she has not the ability as to handle a simple problem such as a simple sensory distorter-- Not even a good one, if I might say, then she is of little value in the big picture."

"Big Picture—Little Picture... Who cares about pictures. I just care about getting out of this garden."

"Yes I see that, and as long as that and other personal smallness holds you in thrall, you will ever be a prisoner. You see my little darling-- This is your problem-- Until you are able to see the universe in all its complexities with a very different vision and perspective than you presently seem to enjoy... You will be imprisoned by your own smallness... FOREVER."

"Forever?" Circe asked suspiciously.

"Yes, Forever," replied the Old One sagely.

"Define forever," came the simple command from Circe.

The well spluttered and hissed.

"Just as I thought. Big threats…. With little meaning. And let me tell you, I am getting real tired of all the steaming and stinky old sputtering coming out of the well when things aren't going your way. Well I have figured out what Forever is, and I also know that you have NOT A CLUE what forever means."

"Do you really know what Forever means?" the Old One asked his old voice thick with feeling.

"Yes I do, and if you treat me in a more civilized manner, maybe, and I only mean MAY--BE, I will explain it to you."

The Old One was overjoyed at what he was hearing. Could it be that **HIS** charge would be the One with the true insight.

MARPLES

Marples sat in front of his largest console, deep within the bowels of his defunct Starcruiser.

MACH FINITUM had been the pride of earth. She had been the culmination of Earth technology. All Nations had been united in her building. She had been the great catalyst that had caused Earth's first peace—ever!

And now the finest achievement of earth's greatest scientific community lay crippled forever with her top six flight stages driven into rock and lake Rha-Adium lapping at her sleek black hide.

If Marples had an inkling of time as time was conceived by Circe in her Garden; then he would know that the circle had opened and closed many times since his crash. Enough time in the "Big Picture," as The Old One put it, to allow Earth to now be in a stage

175

where the wheel had yet to be discovered.

In any picture, Marples ancestors had become his ancestors many times over, and still were.

Marples had an emitter that counted a given amount of emissions over a given period. Counting light emanations had become his way of calculating his concept of time.

And by his most scientific calculations he would live on Rhapour long past his emitter wearing out or his computer being able to compute.

Marples knew that he was doomed to live forever. Whatever "Forever" meant.

Right now, Marples had a problem with his very capable computer. It had just let a life force through twenty three traps, before grinding it to a full stop in the Limbo Lock.

He was busy asking his best friend TC, (short form for Technical Computer) how the entity could have got by twenty three Hypno-Destabalizing-Holos, without being totally ensnared and carted to his command post by his all-purpose-cart--The sagyr.

"It is most difficult to analyze without all relevant data, but from information returned from mobile HDH units one through twenty three, the data returned clearly indicates they have been scanned by a powerful force."

"Are you sure your tubes are all tightened down TC? We are talking about a living organism here, and a small one at that. How could it debrief 23 sophisticated HDH mobiles. If you rolled in on wheels they could even find a phobia that you would respond to, without having to hit you with 23 random shots before getting the right one," Marples said to his 25 story friend that had its black prow buried six stories deep in the rocky beach of Rha-Adium Lake.

"Accusing me of being a prehistoric thing-a-majig that has tubes and such for components is not kind, Marples. How would you like to be referred to as a hairy Neanderthal? Think it over."

"I believe an apology is in order."

Marples had noticed for the last few centuries that his big friend was becoming a trifle crotchety. TC was the most advanced computer ever introduced in Nipponia. How could a computer change?

Computers were a constant factor.... Not subject to change. . .

Was TC damaged? Marples wondered. "Appears to me, you could use a little R &R. What say TC?"

"R &R... I'll give you a little R &R. I'd settle for getting my foreparts extracted from this beach," TC replied with false indignation.

"You know on earth we had a structure much like yourself TC."

"Not in my memory banks you didn't," TC replied.

"Sure we did. And it was even one of the Seven Modern Wonders of my time," Marples said, mischievously.

TC felt the mischief in Marples voice and decided to deprive Marples of the pleasure of an answer.

"Don't you want to know what it was?" Marples said grinning.

"Not especially. But I see you are determined to tell me."

"Well it really wasn't a computerized deep space probe, like you, but it existed without falling over, and it did so at the same impossible angle that you do."

"And from this illogical data you find a comparison?" TC asked, with a slight sneer in her otherwise musical voice.

"Don't you?" Marples replied, knowing that TC was just slightly miffed, at being compared to a poorly constructed building that defied gravity for centuries by not falling over.

"You compare me to a poorly located building that would never have been of any importance, if not for the fact that it was falling over. Well I can think of a few comparisons for you.

And I would indeed tell you of them if I wasn't a lady," TC replied. "But right now we have a problem, as I see the Sagyr has a passenger that is impenetrable. My strongest scanning reveals nothing. All I can determine is a strong physical presence."

"Describe it," Marples told TC.

"Describe it... Now isn't that a master--to-machine command. You sure have nerve Marples, Part-time friend, but, full-time man over machine," TC replied nicely.

Marples knew he was going to pay for his uncomplimentary remark about her being like a leaning tower of unthinking stone. He knew better than to tamper with her vanity, but it was one of his few entertainments. She was the only unpredictable intelligence he had to communicate with.

Until now! For it seemed that the Sagyr was toting a very unpredictable life force. Good. . . Good... Marples thought to himself in anticipation...

TC on the other hand was busy assisting her HDA limbo unit.

"May as well be scanning a rock," TC told Marples.

"Are you sure it isn't some type of advanced mechanical probe?"

"It's a probe all right. But not mechanical. And just what culture on this mud-ball do you suppose could have the technology to build any kind of probe? Never mind a probe sophisticated enough to scramble a powerful HDH scanning unit."

"Just trying to be helpful."

"Then get ready to intercept, as the probe is on its way home. And it's carrying a life force of unknown capabilities."

"Then set up a sequence for containment."

" Physical- or temporal?"

"Strictly physical. Use the magna tractors. Set their power at full traction. That should be enough power to drag a mountain away, or suck a star cruiser out of orbit."

"Your wish is my command--Master," TC replied, obviously not letting go of the leaning tower insult.

The Sagyr came out of the gorge, followed by the HDH unit, its beam at full broadcast, and it's chemical charge depleted.

"It appears all your units have captured is a small girl," Marples accused TC.

"So it would appear," said TC.

"Do you suggest she is other than she appears?"

"Why would I suggest anything?"

"How about a truce?" Marples said sincerely... TC noted the sincerity and immediately responded in like fashion. After all, she was merely a pre-programmed computer that had been perfectly tailored to his psyche profile. . . How else for a commander of a Deep space Star Cruiser to remain even relatively sane...

And she was only a technical computer.

At least in the beginning she was.

A STRANGE VALLEY

"My what a lovely place," Rhaeve said, sitting up.

"Who are you?" asked Marples.

"What are YOU?" Boomed the great voice of TC, Not feminine now. NO... This voice was one of deep masculine authority.

"Who I am is easy. I am the Rhaeve of Rha," Rhaeve spoke in her best little-girl voice.

"As to--What I am... "

The overhead sky was bright and sunny, but even as Rhaeve spoke black clouds rolled ominously over the valley. Sheet lightning filled the valley, accompanied by terrible winds that howled down through the valley. Clap after clap of thunder, became stronger--Reverberating--Rhaeve... Rhaeve... Rhaeve...

"I am the RHAEVE OF THE UNIVERSE," a terrible voice rumbled high in the skies, bringing down a deluge of water, a greater show of forked lightning accompanied by thunder, and more water followed. The skies seemed to growl down on the very spot where the Starcruiser lay buried in the stone.

"How's that for theatrics--You big phony," Rhaeve laughed up at the black gleaming hull. "Imagine a great thinking entity, such as yourself, trying to intimidate a being my size. Such insecurity is hard to conceive. And sending a mobile Hypno-drug-hologram unit to hunt down helpless beings ... Tsk... Tsk... Tsk..." Rhaeve said, scrutinizing the discomforted Marples, unfathomable from behind her always closed eyes.

"No harm was done," Marples said.

"If there had been. I'd bring this valley down around the heads of both you near-morons," Rhaeve said, with conviction in her small voice.

"I have never harmed a living creature," Marples said.

What powers can you wield to threaten a Starcruiser?" The very well equipped computer thought at Rhaeve.

If a starship could be deemed to shudder. . . TC did.

"You really are the Rhaeve," TC broadcast aloud.

"Old Dervisal Predictions. . . True!" Marples said, in awe.

"Not a doubt about it. Every factor fits. She is the wildcard the Great Mother has been waiting for," TC said.

Rhaeve thought of her own existence as she briefly knew of it, and yes, she could be described as a wild card, as to where she had slept, and why, and how long, was not within being described as a wild entity, rather it was an entity of non being yet she knew her purpose was quickly starting to unravel, and she could clearly see that this now defunct starship, and it's captain, held many keys to padlocks she was shortly to unlock. . .

Possibly. . . .

"Which of you two beings is the master? And who is servant?" Rhaeve asked, innocently.

The silent mind thoughts that passed quickly between TC and Marples brought tears of mirth to Rhaeve's forever closed eyes.

Rhaeve could clearly see that in their symbiotic state of inter-dependence, neither being had thought of itself as either master or servant. It was clear to Rhaeve that they had existed here as friends that respected and needed each other. She could understand the man-made computer needing Marples, as the great black sentient creature had been tailored for him, but for a relationship to grow and change was a concept well worth looking into much deeper. . . For if a man-machine relationship could affect changes, then she of unbridled

powers could certainly do no less...
She only needed to know the way.

And Rhaeve knew she could learn a
great deal of the way of learning--
from this insignificant sized life form
known as Marples. She knew that the
glistening black machine held much
data valuable to her, but Rhaeve
knew that locked tight in the mind of
Marples was information that would
help her reach her true destiny. She
knew it was not so much data she
craved as direction.

And direction could only be arrived at
by an intelligence that also had the
ability to elect choices without all data
being in place at the point of election.
Rhaeve could see that in spite of its
enormous ability to contain
information, TC had not the capacity
for making a choice between
unknown variables. If all known
factors were not in place, she could
see that TC could draw no
conclusions.

Marples on the other hand was a
creature that could make selections

without knowing consciously the reasoning....

Rhaeve knew that it would take this type of wild, almost random choice selecting, that was done without volition. These were the thought patterns that had no limitations. And she knew that this was to be her way.

And she knew she could learn the way from Marples only.

"Marples my friend, for you are going to be my friend Marples. Do you have trouble with this?" Rhaeve said, coyly.

"Great!" Marples told TC, "straddled with an adolescent of unquestionable powers. Hope she isn't given to violence, or fancies of flight. Or reading my mind uninvited."

Rhaeve stared at him, waiting for an answer,

"Well, are you reading my mind?" asked Marples.

"No. I respect privacy. Unless you want a mind-linking?"

"Why do I feel that your coming to this valley is no accident?"

"Because you have spoken of me with Thragg, and Thragg knew that I would be coming here."

"It's true that I have spoken with Thragg, with the help of my good friend TC I might add."

"Then you admit speaking with Thragg about me?"

"Not you as a person, but we speculated as to his being bound to the Tree for so long... And your coming was expected. Actually, TC has become a good friend to Thragg," Marples said, looking to his small hands, that he was rubbing together, nervously.

"There is no need to fear me. I have come not to hurt you. I seek only information," Rhaeve said, gently.

"I know why you are here, I have been expecting you for a long, long, long, time..."

"How could you know of my coming? If not from Thragg""

"The Great Sleeping Mother has occasionally scanned TC to see if you had made an appearance at the Tree. She never speaks to me, for that matter, she never speaks directly to TC. More like she invades like a swarm of ants, taking information she wants and leaving poor TC in a state of near mental exhaustion. If TC was a lesser entity, she would have long ago expired from these invasions, but she is made of stern stuff is good old TC, and she weathers these avalanches of her inner being."

"You don't sound as if you like the Great Mother."

"I don't. But I am a limited human being caught up with all things personal. It's the only way I can respond. We humans are not complicated, nor far-seeing, and I don't pretend to understand a life force that appears logical to the point of being inconsiderate. . . And often cruel. Not caring seems to be her most likable attitude. If she cared about nothing she would sleep forever, and that might be better than cruel. But then I am only a small pawn in this game, and have little understanding of major entities."

"You belittle yourself. I understand from Thragg that you have been kidnapping people for thousands of years. . . That sounds like a major player to me."

"Were it my plan, and if I performed it of my own volition, then I might be construed as a player," Marples replied.

"And you're not free?" Rhaeve challenged.

"Oh... I am free enough," Marples laughed without humor.

"Then you must be counted a player," Rhaeve insisted.

"Not in the way you mean it."

"Why not?"

"Well this task I perform is not my idea."

"Who's idea then?" Rhaeve badgered on.

"The clearest picture that I can grasp, seems to involve a swirling life force that has but one thought," Marples answered.

"And that is?"

"It is not entirely clear to me, but it seems to involve getting the Great Mother to awaken, so that she may continue her journey."

"Why is she asleep?" Rhaeve asked, not expecting an answer to such an important question.

"If I could answer that question, then I would know the prime problem for all off-worlders that are on Rhapour."

"Do you have the answer?" Rhaeve asked, already knowing that Marples knew the secret of the Sleeping.

Thragg had told Rhaeve about Marples at their first mind-linking. Thragg hadn't been given the information, but he knew that it would be given freely to Rhaeve.

"Yes I have the whole story," Marples said.

"Thragg has led me to believe that you may be a friend to me. He further believes that you should be my mentor. Why would he think that you, a mere mortal could be a mentor to a Rhaeve?"

"Possibly because I have the answers that you need. Come...Let's leave this dark place. We can walk along the lake, and I will tell you how the Great Mother became involved. And how we all wound up on this planet," Marples said, taking the small hand of his protégé in his own small hand, and leading her out of the ship into the bright light of day.

"Isn't this better for you?" Marples asked.

"If you have been selected to be my mentor, then you already have the answer to your own question," Rhaeve said.

They squeezed hands in mutual happiness.

"You don't have to hold my hand you know. I can see just fine without the use of my eyes."

"Are they damaged?" Marples asked.

"No. . . My eyes are fine, but to open them is death for all around me. Did you not know this already?"

"No, I didn't know that your sight was that of the Old Ones. I thought that you had the control they lack."

"Oh I have control, but in the presence of fragile life forces I must keep my vision bridled."

"It is vision that can take---or give life. And you are never to be a taker of life. You are the bringer of change. So I can only guess that your sight is the wild magic that will bring the Great Mother to life again," Marples said, stopping to take a small stone from his sandal.

"Come sit here beside me on this log," Marples told Rhaeve, as he took off his sandal and washed the small cut in his foot.

"Is the lake not death to you Marples?"

"No... It is in fact the secret to my being still alive after twenty thousand years. The life allotment on my planet is no greater than for that of a Rhapourian."

"Yes, hard radiation is death to most, but to others it is the key to what you would call immortality," Rhaeve agreed.

"Although I have lived longer than any other from my planet, I often find it to be less than a blessing," Marples said, with just a trace of sadness in his voice.

"Do you miss your own kind?" Rhaeve asked.

"Sometimes- -And you?"

"I don't know any of my kind... I don't know if there are any other of my kind. Do you have an answer to this?"

"No, but what TC and I have deduced, is that you are the first ever of the line of Rhaeve. You are to be a greater Mother in your own right, even greater than She Who Sleeps."

"Am I to be as powerful?"

"No. Nothing in the known universe has the power, of the Great One. Her powers are beyond even imagining. And that takes us to your original question, as to why she is asleep, and why, with all her power's, she needs your help," Marples said, lacing his sandal on again.

"Then you a mere mortal have the answer to the greatest problem ever to beset this galaxy. The ways of the universe are strange indeed," Rhaeve mused.

"I know the cause of the problem better than anything I will ever understand, for I am the problem," Marples said, simply.

"You... A mere mortal are the cause of the Mother's state?"

"Yes. It was an accident some twenty thousand years ago, and it happened in deep space. How we all became wrecked on this planet is not for me to know. TC, with her incredible powers of memory and analysis can only speculate how we all came to this far end of an untraveled galaxy."

"But why does the Mother sleep?" asked Rhaeve.

"She is sleeping until you fulfill your mission, then she will leave this galaxy to its own destiny. Even now, she is not interfering with the inhabitants of this planet, nor any other living creatures in this galaxy."

"You mean she is helpless to leave this galaxy?"

"Yes, it seems that without the star charts which are so deeply locked in the unfathomable mind of Thragg, She has no idea where her universe is located. And she has not the right to interfere with her sisters in their galaxies."

"So much power, and yet so helpless. It is difficult to believe she is trapped just because she is unable to navigate her way home."

"Difficult to believe or not... She is trapped until you solve her dilemma... If you can," Marples replied with doubt showing in his small voice.

"Is navigation her only problem?"

"No, but if it was, it would be enough to leave her stranded here forever. Without Thragg being in full power as a Navigator, The Great Pyramind that engulfs the Mother in deep space would have no known co-ordinates to project to. And that would leave the Pyramind stranded in deep space forever.... And then there would be no possible salvation from limbo. Limbo forever would be the destiny of all those that compose the Pyramind."

"What is a Pyramind?" Rhaeve asked, just starting to realize the magnitude of the task before her.

"Ah... The Pyramind. I will tell you all about the Pyramind. And also of the reason why She sleeps. And of why She is here. And how it was an accident not foreseen by her many Great members of the Pyramind. And certainly not of a simple mind such as mine. Even TC is totally blameless....... Morally at least."

All this I will tell you about, as it is required for your development," Marples told the frail being that clutched his hand so tightly. Tightly and with trust.... And Marples was helpless to tell her more until it was required.

"Why can you not tell me more now?" Asked Rhaeve with trust.

"It is not my choosing that tells, or withholds information from you Rhaeve. I am unfree to give you the information you crave so badly until it is needed. Somehow I am only able to inform you on a need to know basis. That is all I can see by looking within with my limited introspective powers. If you want, I will drop all barriers and you can plumb my memory to your fullest. Yet, somehow, I feel that you will gain nothing by approaching the problem from this direction. The mind power of the Old One in the garden lays heavy on this area of my mind, and I don't believe even you can force your way past his barriers set in my mind. At least you can't do it yet... The future will unravel as it will. But never mind all of that for now. Come and visit with all those I have kidnapped."

"Are they all in this little valley?" asked Rhaeve.

"All except, those that refuse to obey the laws of the valley," Marples said, waving to two small children.

"Are there many laws?" Rhaeve asked.

"Just two."

"And they are?"

"The first law is the one that governs all living entities that live within the confines of the Great Mother. You already know this law of Empathy."

"Yes I know that all living things must not commit any act they would not want committed against themselves. But what is the second law of this valley?" Rhaeve asked.

"You should have been named—She who asks too many questions, but to answer your question. The second law of this valley is that no couple can have more children than two."

"That should keep the population at a zero growth rate."

"Actually it is a rate of declension not growth. For some couples do not have even two children. Some are childless, others are content to have only one child. Then some are taken by the lake. Carelessness near the lake brings almost instant death for a child."

"What if a couple has more than two children?" Rhaeve asked.

"Instant banishment to the Shadow forest is their fate."

"For breaking of either law?"

"Yes."

"Seems harsh."

"It's the law of the Old Ones from the Garden."

"Are there any exceptions?"

"None. The laws are simple, but strict. And they're not my laws, so don't look at me like that," Marples said, defensively.

They came to a waist high, fruit-bearing hedge.

"This is the border that those of the valley are not permitted to cross. All the other side is safe from contamination. Come through and meet these prisoners of mine," Marples said, grinning broadly.

About five hundred spotlessly white adobe homes formed the hub of each farm. The flat cup of the valley was bare of even one building, but the gentle slopes of the valley had been terraced into ten acre farms. From high up in the mountainous part of the valley, a bubbling brook had been tapped, bringing sparkling water through a simple open duct system to each farm.

"On my planet we would call this prison Utopia," Marples said, with Pride in his voice.

"Utopia? And what does Utopia mean," Rhaeve asked.

"In the fifteenth century on my planet Sir Thomas More, described the perfect social and political life for all humans. And this is as close as it gets to that ideal state, this prison of mine," Marples laughed.

"But if you force people to accept your concept of even an ideal state, it is still wrong," Rhaeve challenged.

"I agree, but, this valley has a tunnel that leads into the Shadow forest, and any that want to leave, can. As a matter of fact, the Elders leave the valley when they have learned enough to pass on their knowledge to their primitive brothers. And occasionally a primitive comes through the tunnel to live with us for a while. Some stay--Some return. All of their own volition."

"What of those from the Tree?"

"It has been chopped for over a hundred years. That is why our population is small."

"If this utopian concept is so great, why do you not make it possible for all?" Rhaeve asked coyly.

"It is... For it is only a way of living, and has absolutely nothing to do with this valley," Marples replied.

Three children approached. Two wore long white robes, and were happily throwing an open circle back and forth. The third wore only a loin cloth, and his small body glistened like oiled ebony. His huge gray eyes were flecked with gold and mischief.

"Hello Marples the Magnificent. How is your munificent lord this splendid day," came a sing-song voice from the ebony child.

"Pookergee. . .Pookergee. And how are you this splendid day yourself-- You rascal you. Are you keeping out of mischief Pook? Or is that too much to wish for," Marples said, his apple-like face, breaking into a wide grin.

"And is this wondrous creature a princess?" Pookergee said, in pretended awe.

"As a matter of fact she is just that very thing."

"A real princess?" Pookergee asked, not sure if he was being put-on by Marples or not. Deciding Rhaeve was too young to be a princess, he approached her as bold as only a ten year old can be. "Pleased to meetcha your royal highness," he said.

"I'm not a royal anything. But you may call me Rhaeve, and I will call you Pooky. Is that all right by you?" Rhaeve asked, showing small even teeth in a dazzling gesture of friendship.

"Okey-dokey by Pookergee. You have nice voice, maybe Pookergee will marry to you some time. You call me Pook now, by and by, you call me Love," he roared, rolling his gray eyes till only the whites showed.

"Marples, I think I will have Pook show me around if he will," Rhaeve told Marples in a very positive manner.

"Is this ok with you Pookergee?" Marples asked.

"Okey-dokey with me." Pookergee agreed heartily, all the time hopping around Rhaeve, and all the time wagging his head from side to side and making funny faces for his instant friend.

Marples left to greet a great white giant of a woman and her small yellow male companion, and their two children who tugged them in the direction of Marples.

Pookergee ran around Rhaeve singing:

> *MARRY TO ME*
> *MARRY TO ME*
>
> *COME SEE   COME SEE*
> *COME SEE   COME SEE*
> *PRETTY TO QUEEN*
> *PRETTY TO QUEEN*

MARRY TO ME
MARRY TO ME

GOLDEN QUEEN
GOLDEN QUEEN
COME SEE   *COME SEE*
COME SEE   *COME SEE*

"I see that big Mioola and her family want to talk. Pookergee is a bright lad, he will show you anything you need to know about my prison," Marples said, leaving Rhaeve in the capable hands of her little consort.

"What to see first?" Pookergee said, taking Rhaeve's small golden hand in his smaller black one.

"You don't have to hold my hand. I can see fine," Rhaeve told her beaming little ten year old escort.

"Pook like to hold it. Like to touch it!" he grinned rubbing her arm with his other hand.

"Love to touch it!" he sung to himself, glowing with pride.

"You sure are an affectionate rascal." Rhaeve said, rubbing his little head with her free hand.

Hand and hand they spent the day wandering through the many gardens, drinking the sparkling water and eating some of the ripe fruit that grew along the path.

That night a huge cook-fire was held in the circular meadow. As the guest of honor, and a newcomer to the valley, Rhaeve was introduced to all. Rhaeve could not help but notice that the yellows, browns, whites, and the gray eyed blacks, were all intermarried. There was no color barriers in the valley. Thomas More's fabled island of utopia could have not been as idyllic.

"I notice that there is no meat," Rhaeve said, to Marples.

"No, we eat not of the flesh of animals, nor do we wear their skins. No animals die here because of us," Marples replied.

"Tomorrow I spend the day with TC, then I must leave in search of where the great calling is to be held. I now know most of my task ahead. After a day with TC I am sure I'll have a few more answers to questions long unanswered, and before I leave, you will tell me why the Mother sleeps," Rhaeve told Marples sternly.

THE GARDEN

"Living Death! Come up so I can smell your breath. Bring the stench of brimstone and I'll talk to you like the fool you believe me to be, but hurry now, the Rhaeve is finally learning to stay in the sunlight where she will not keep falling asleep. I truly wonder what imbecile forgot to build in some defense against her being trapped in the land of sleep. Everyone seems to use sleep as a cure-all to their problems. You sleep. My mother sleeps. Rhaeve is but a child, and she sleeps. The master planner certainly had a thing for sleeping. Come up right now or I will draw you up with or without your consent," Circe said into the well, with ominous authority.

"Not sniveling as usual?" teased the Old One, coming out of the well without his usual fanfare of burning stench.

"I expect a whole lot of respect out of you from this day forward, for you are a worm and I am the soon-to-be Mother. This Galaxy will be mine to rule, and the first thing I will do is make sure you and your three other selves take a powder."

"Where are your pretty feathers?" the Old One asked, in false servility, attempting to mollify the obviously growing monster.

"Birds have feathers fool--Do I look like a bird?"

"Great Gods, help us all. She is changing, and into, a monster I fear," thought the Old One to himself.

"Good! I see that I have your full attention for a change. Now you sit and listen, for your days in the well as you have falsely represented **IT**, are over."

"OH My! Your new scales are so lovely," toadied the Old One.

"Yes they are, and they are arrow and spear proof, I might add, and not to the delight of the miserable savages that live at the Garden's edge. For thousands of years the fore fathers of these heathens have been making my life one of extreme misery. . .Never again. They will soon be erecting idols in my image to bow down to. As the miserable vermin should!" Circe declared, rising up on her great clawed hind legs, and leering down threateningly at the Old One from her height of over twenty feet, each scale gleaming, and her small leathery wings tucked tight against her body.

"The only thing I miss from my former self is the ability to fly. These little wings are worthless to the new me," Circe complained to the Old One.

"Soon you will fly as you can't begin to imagine. Yours will be a flight through the galaxy," promised the Old One.

"Yes, but before my Mother can continue to her galaxy, and before many wrongs can be put right, she who sees without sight must be helped in her quest of waking my mother."

"I agree that it appears as if the Rhaeve needs help, but I assure you there is nothing that can be done by any but her."

"I am strong now. I could help," declared the young dragon.

"No, your time is not yet come. Soon come. Soon come....MY beautiful child. For as powerful as you are destined to be. You are still child to me. Even as your magnificent mother is child to me. Greater in stature she is without question... But also always a child," the Old One's voice swirled around Circe like a myriad of stars, clustering and clouding her vision. Soon her vision cleared and the Old One was still sitting deep in his supposed well, smiling up happily at his young charge.

"All right you've made your point. So I still have a lot to learn, but you are not to talk to me as you did when I was a withering flying thing."

"Agreed!" the Old One almost shouted. "But come here and sit beside the well and look into this pool of water."

"Why?" came the suspicious reply of the young dragon.

"There are things you must be taught, now that you are so rapidly developing. And always remember not to touch me."

"Why? If I am going to be so darned powerful... How come I still can't touch you? Almost forever I wasn't allowed to look directly at you, well that is no longer a problem, except that you are truly ugly, but you are no longer a danger to look at. Why are you still a danger to the touch?"

"Because I am hard radiation in a form that will always be death for you and your kind. Only the Rhaeve can walk freely through my being and live. . . Only the Rhaeve, that is why she is so important. For the power of her eyes will bring the Mother to life, and only the Orca can guide us back to our galaxy. Only the Rhaeve can enter his mind without killing him. If I or your Mother were to even touch his mind--The Master Navigator would die a terrible death, leaving your Mother stranded in this uncharted galaxy forever. And I know you have a better picture of what forever is than I could imagine. So be careful in all you do, or you could do irreparable damage to the fabric of this galaxy."

"It is frightening," declared the young dragon.

"Certainly it's frightening. But if you tamper with anything you could leave the Great Pyramind stranded here for what you know forever to be. So tamper with nothing! Do you understand?"

"I Do, I Do," replied Circe seeing the picture clear for the first time ever.

Good. Then sit down and let's get to the business at hand."

"Which is?" Queried Circe with real respect in her voice, also for the first time ever.

"We can't help the Rhaeve directly, for only she can make a positive change in this galaxy. When you come into your own, then you can make changes in this galaxy, but right now you would only be murdered by the savages. For they truly fear dragons. If you think being a flying feathered thing was dangerous, you have no idea how perilous life can be. Every warrior would turn against you in fear and anger. And all with lance or ax."

"That is extremely unfair! I can't even defend myself against violence what good are my new powers to be, if I can't protect myself against savages?" Circe howled with impotent rage.

Now you are beginning to see why Rhaeve is so important. She can protect herself without having to resort to violence."

"But she has the option of violence?" asked Circe.

"I hope we do not find out," replied the Old One, darkly.

IN SEARCH OF THE CALLING

Marples and Rhaeve walked back to his crippled Starcruiser in silence. Both deep in thought.

"Now that you have seen my valley, do you still call me kidnaper?" Marples asked, knowing the answer by the smile on Rhaeve's golden face.

"No, for I see that you had no more option in your destiny, than gentle Thragg, and none could fault Thragg."

"Do you want to hear about the events that led up to my star cruiser and the pyramind being stranded here for twenty thousand years?" Marples asked.

"No, but I will spend the next day or so with TC, then if I have any questions, I'll ask. Right now, I don't have enough information to ask valid questions," Rhaeve said, sitting down on a rock and washing her feet in the glowing lake.

"It really kills."

Rhaeve laughed absent mindedly. "Yes I know it does, but hard radiation is no danger to me. What puzzles me is how a fragile being such as yourself does not perish in it." Rhaeve swirled her feet in the life giving-taking water. "Don't approach me again until I rise from this stone. For if you do I will give you great pain. I have much to learn from your friend TC, and I want no interruptions. Do you understand?" Rhaeve said

"No I don't understand, but I'll not bother you."

"Good—Now go." Rhaeve commanded sternly.

For three days Marples was unable to access his great black friend. The master console remained blank, regardless of his attempts to activate TC. For three days Marples wandered about the village like a balloon in the wind. Finally Rhaeve got up from the stone, her small, already golden, body glowing with ten times the brilliance of the lake.

"Marples you must come with me, for the time grows short, and it will be long before it becomes right again," Rhaeve told Marples.

The master screen lit up and TC joined in, "You must accompany Rhaeve my good friend, but have no fears, this questing that Rhaeve is compelled to journey on, needs your assistance. And soon it will be over."

"Where do we go?" asked Marples, concerned about leaving the valley that had been so safe and snug and predictable for twenty thousand years.

"We go in search of the place of the calling. For all things are known to me, and I must now just fit the pieces back together as best I can."

"Do you mean you can make TC whole again?" Marples asked hopefully.

"No... I am not a magi. Anyway you would have nowhere to go, for the planet you know as earth is no longer. Your home is here for as long as you choose to live, or until the level of radiation becomes too feeble to support life... And I can dry up Rha Adium lake any time you wish, so that option is always open to you," Rhaeve said, gently touching his arm.

"Suicide?" Marples asked, looking to Rhaeve in disbelief.

"Sleep, Quiet untroubled sleep," Rhaeve corrected. "But come now, let us not dwell on it. We have many tasks to accomplish before the black hole is as it was when the accident took place."

"Then you know why the Mother sleeps?"

"I know everything," was Rhaeve's reply, not a boast, just a statement of fact.

"Then you know the guilt I have carried all these years?"

"The fault was not yours, nor was it the fault of Thragg, although his feeling of guilt is as yours. . ."

"And that is?" Marples asked, his voice heavy with guilt.

"Unfounded, stupid, without Reason! It was an accident, and nothing more! If there was any fault it was that of the Great Mother, for it was her that was asleep at the lip of the black gate. She better understood the black hole than your computer or her pyramind crew. In spite of this she elected to sleep on the lip of power. Waiting the next tide flow, right on a lip of power, is extremely dangerous. She knew this. You on the other hand still have no true picture of what a hole is. And although Thragg was the Master Navigator of the great pyramind, the Mother commanded him to use the critical power of the lip for her return journey. How could she know that just stepping through the gate of her galaxy for a short period, would precipitate an accident— because a primitive Starcruiser would be drawing power from the very same gate for a push through its own galaxy. If there was any fault it was the Mother—Or the Old Ones."

"Then I have felt guilt for all these years for nothing?"

"Just that simple... You are guilty of nothing, and neither is Thragg. The only guilt you both share is the guilt of having a feeling of greater self importance than either of you are."

"Have you told Thragg?"

"Certainly."

"And?" Marples asked, excitedly.

"Thragg is free finally. I am not letting him return through the black hole. He has suffered enough. He has a family and new responsibilities, soon his legs and arms will be no more, and he will enjoy life as it was intended for him. And never more will the old sloot put her mind grasp upon a gentle orca and warp such a gentle creature into deep space. Though deep space be a place of comfort for the Mother... It is a misery for most."

"How can you—the Rhaeve, who is sworn to serve and respect the Great Mother—Speak so?"

"Little do you know of who serves and who commands in the greater picture my little friend… But it is enough to say that she is a great lazy sloot that caused all this by her sleeping, and if she finds fault with this we will see who is who!"

Marples felt an uncontrollable fear that caused his flesh to crawl around on his bones.

"I don't understand the way of powers. But I just had a terrible feeling that you are not as you seem," Marples blurted.

Rhaeve laughed coldly.

"Whatever I am, even I am not a dealer in magic, and even my wishes are not necessarily commands to inanimate objects. But with imagination, desire, a little power, and finally, the right information, possibly, I can set this accident in order. Although I have little regard for the Great Mother, her role in her galaxy is one of supreme importance, for she has one single beautifully redeeming quality," Rhaeve told Marples, "and that is that she will tolerate no discord around her. Her mother before her was a sloot, and her mother before her…. But they have all been peaceful sloots that tolerated no warring within their domain. And if her galaxy wasn't on the brink of inter-planetary warfare I would let the old sloot sleep. But waken her I must, for she has much work to do in her own galaxy. I may even go for the ride just to watch the Old Demon whip her galaxy into shape. My genes tell me she is a terrifying MOTHER when she is angry."

"Select a stout stick my friend, and heavy boots, for we are about to do a great deal of walking in search of the Calling."

"I gather neither TC nor Thragg had the co-ordinates of the Pyramind's crash," Marples said, removing his sandals and replacing them with solid hemp boots.

"No. TC has never had the information and Thragg is damaged so badly that his best recall is worth little. Fortunately he had the location of his first officer aboard the Pyramind. And a great blue troll should be easy to find."

"Agreed," Marples grinned, happy that Rhaeve was returning to what he considered to be normal. The hard minded being that had been speaking through her lips had been one not of Marples liking.

THE SHADOW

They walked through the tunnel into the Shadow Forest. Bozark the brown, King of the Shadow, Lord of all True Men on Rhapour, drew deeply on his hookhash pipe, sending the thick pungent smoke into swirling clouds around his golden head.

"What do you see?" Blewitt, the three foot, blue troll asked, looking up from his own cloud of blue smoke, that he was busy forming into the female form of a pink troll.

"Fancy a pink one do you," Bozark leered, good naturedly.

"Fancy anything other than those great mindless monsters that I am saddled with. God but they are ugly. I mean how would you like to fornicate with a thirty foot pile of stone?"

"For an old man... You sure get preoccupied with sex," Bozark grinned, sending a yellow female puff of smoke into the air over Blewitt's head.

"Fancy that color?" Bozark chuckled, tears running down his golden brown cheeks.

"What's this?" Bozark said, looking to the picture that was forming in his cloud.

"Looks like that pesky little Marples is bringing a guest. She looks like one of your kind. Look her skin is glowing a lot Brighter than yours. Think she is a relation?" Blewitt asked seriously.

"Can't be. All that have even a touch of the True Rhanians Lords live in the Shadow. Never seen one that glowed like this one. There has been talk of a strange girl appearing and disappearing around Fishfind. They claim her strange."

"The one that claims to be the last of Rha?" asked the troll, cutting in on Bozark's thoughts.

"Could be her. She sure is unbelievably pretty."

"Better you stick to fantasizing about trolls Blewitt."

"Fantasizing be damned. I was just thinking about tales told in Nod about a blind child that created the Oasis of Bhola,"

"Whatever the truth of the story. The True of Rha were all males. You were aboard their ship when it crashed into the metal tank of Marples. What were the real princes like Blewitt?"

"They was cold fish they was," Blewitt said, drawing a great throat full of blue smoke and sending it into the fading scene of Rhaeve and Marples. "But they was kind of heart, and blind, and their appearance was much like the girl in the sworlings."

"How so?" asked Bozark.

"Well for one thing, they was blind. And that girl sure appears blind. They glowed like her. Course they was taller. There is one big big problem with her being a descendant, or you

being one either.... for that matter,"
Blewitt speculated.

"What problem?"

"Well they had no children. That sort of wrecks the theory of you, or her, or anyone being descended from them," Blewitt laughed, then blew an extra thick load of smoke into his vision.

"You mean they had no known descendants here."

"Nope . . . I mean they never had children ever."

"That's a stupid theory. If they had no children ever, and their parents before them had no children... How do you suppose they came to be?" Bozark laughed.

"Just tellin' what I know to be fact. And I know for certain they never had children. When an old prince become tired in spirit he would simply clone an exact replica of himself. Now with this in mind how do you think you could be related. . . And even more impossible--How could a girl be cloned from a male?"

"I didn't know that. How come you never told me before now?"

"Didn't want to hurt your feelings and all. But I traveled with those stuffy princes on many the journey. And most of them never lived over thirty thousand years before feeling the need to clone themselves."

"And then?"

"And then they took the Sleep. Same as those cantankerous dragons." Blewitt grinned, changing his picture back into a female troll.

"You have kept that secret from me all these years, and I always thought you to be a good and true friend," Bozark accused.

"Ahh well! As to being a good and true friend--Why would a friend bring hard cold miserable facts into a friendly gab while we was enjoying the toke of a friendly pipe. Hard truth can freeze up a warm happening between friends. Leave it alone good friend."

Blewitt looked long and thoughtful at the scene moving through the blue cloud. "She sure has the look of those proud devils," he said, letting the scene dissolve.

As the word traveled ahead, that a true princess of Rha was searching throughout the Shadow for the Great Blue Troll.

Blewitt fled to the land of the Dervisals

With the coming of Rhaeve and Marples in his great Magi coat and conical hat, the Shadow was alive with dreams being passed back and forth by the Truemen of the Shadow. The talking hook hash pipes were busy following the apparent mindless meandering of the blind child and the Magnificent Marples. No approach was made to hamper or guide their journey. But the watching pipes smoked heavily on the passage of these two foreign things in the domain of Truemen.

Rhaeve read the sworlings and took Marples out of the misty hazings of the Shadow Forest and into the land of the Dervisals. For she could see that the Great Blue Troll was on the move with definite purpose. And that purpose was to take his four great stone girls to the place of the Calling.

Rhaeve and Marples sat in front of a small smoldering fire, eating the last of the beans Marples had brought in his magicians ruck-sack. "It's to be a cold night Rhaeve," Marples said, inching just a little closer to the fire. "Lots of room in my great coat for both of us," Marples said, adding more wet wood to the already struggling fire.

"I'm never cold. But I'm sorry that I have not been attuned to your needs. I have been trying to communicate with the Blue Troll. And he seems so involved in his own pursuits as to block all my attempts to communicate."

"You are starting to develop long range as well as close up powers?" Marples asked rubbing his almost frozen hands together in attempt at warming them.

"Yes I am getting more range," Rhaeve replied dreamily, her mind busy elsewhere.

"You sure you don't want to share my coat?" Marples offered again, not completely convinced that Rhaeve was warm. She looked so small and helpless sitting cross legged at least twenty feet from the fire. She just sat and stared out into the dark night.

"Come away from the fire, it will only make you sick breathing that poor excuse for a fire."

"It's the best I can build. Can you build better?" Marples asked hopefully. "Fires aren't my best trick," Marples laughed.

"Come sit with your back against mine. Soon you will be warm, and I see that the Dervisal has night creatures on the prowl. I am getting many garbled thought-patterns from the dark, and not all of them are for our well-being. Unless you consider being their dinner a good thought."

With alacrity Marples scurried over to Rhaeve and quickly sat down. Immediately he seated himself, a soft glow emanated from Rhaeve. The glowing formed a soft tent of warmth around them.

"Why did you not do this before?" Marples asked, thinking of all the cold nights he had endured since leaving the protection and warmth of TC and the lake.

"My mind has been on the trail of the troll, and a busy trail he has set for us. I am in the habit of shielding my radiation as it is a sure killer to all living things. I had completely forgotten about your being exposed to it. Now that I am linked to your needs I see that, you not only have the ability to live with it. —You also have the inability to live without it. So for the rest of this journey, we will be as what you know to be Siamese twins."

"If that means staying as warm as I am right now. It suits me just fine!" Marples agreed happily, warm for the first time since leaving his lake.

"It means more than warmth my little friend. It means staying alive!" Rhaeve said, with conviction. "You are not to leave my side, for fear of death. Do you understand?"

"This is pretty heavy conversation. But I do like the warmth," Marples said, stretching with the luxury of warmth.

Marples was soon warm enough to unbutton his multi-colored magi-coat. He spread it out and they both lay on their backs looking up into the starscape.

"Now that I am not miserable from the cold, I can appreciate the night. Thanks," Marples told Rhaeve, being careful not to actually touch the young girl.

"You sure have strange thoughts," Rhaeve said, turning her head to look at Marples with her closed eyes.

"Reading my inner thoughts again?" Marples asked.

"Only to make sure you are not getting too much radiation, nor too little. You have radiation dependency, and I am just matching my aura to yours. And not spying on those strange little thoughts you are so busy trying to repress--and hide from me."

In the dark Marples blushed and shut all boy-girl thoughts from his mind.

Rhaeve chuckled to herself, because of the guilt felt by Marples for thinking perfectly normal thoughts.

"You are truly a proper gentleman," Rhaeve whispered.

Marples moved away another inch, his face more than warm enough to suit him.

Strange harsh grunting noises came from the dark. It was the dreaded language of the Dervisals, and Marples could tell that they encircled the small clearing.

"Never mind them Marples. Just sleep. You are badly rundown. You have been away from your lake for two weeks, and if not for your almost freezing, I wouldn't have realized until too late that you were dying. Sleep now. A good sleep will give you strength to face tomorrow," Rhaeve said, placing her small hand on his forehead, then gently closing his eyes. Marples drifted slowly into the sleep of the near-dead.

Around her Rhaeve could hear the closing in of a very large, well armed party of Dervisals.

She knew they would not attack in the dark, for they were as all savages -- deeply in fear of the unknown. And her presence was to them as if a great demon had fallen into their midst, and it was their fate to face the demon.

THE GARDEN

Blewitt sat high upon the head of the mindless rock troll "Left, right, left, right," he commanded strongly, thinking each instruction as simply as possible, and ever so slowly the great mindless hulk responded--Left, right, left, right, and so the journey started, from deep in the land of the Dervisals. Carefully and without ever breaking the thought of movement, Blewitt guided his vehicle towards the Garden.

Rhaeve and Marples slept a deep sleep. And the Old One and Circe waited in anticipation, for they both knew that, with the coming of the Great Blue Troll, their freedom was near.

"How come that little blue troll is known as The Great Blue Troll?" Circe asked the Old One.

"Because of his Great control, for who but a great power could control and manipulate a mindless creature. This ability makes him great. And as you can plainly see, he is a blue troll, therefore he is known through the galaxies as The Great Blue Troll, for no other being in any galaxy can give life to and control a pile of mindless rock."

"What, about my Mother? Can't she control the stone troll?"

"No. Even your mother has no ability to give a pile of rock a specific command and have the rock respond."

"Can you control it?" asked Circe.

"No. I do have the powers, as indeed your mother, and soon you, to destroy the stone creature, but only the blue troll has the unique power of control over a stone troll," the Old One said, tired of questions.

"You always seemed so awesome to me. Now I see you for what you are... Finally!" uttered Circe, her rich voice thick with contempt.

"If it's any consolation I've always hoped that you would be other than you are," retorted The Old One, coldly.

"I see that you are angry at losing your control over me," Circe replied, sparkling venom dripping and burning the grass.

"As usual you see nothing correctly, and at the Calling I will be informing your great mother that she will have to send another in your place to be the watchdog of this galaxy."

"Watchdog! You call me WATCHDOG!" Circe roared, sending a blast of fire spewing over the verdant garden. The entire Garden lay burnt and black, and in the center the Ahpoo tree stood bright and unscathed by the fire.

"We have failed good friend," the Old One told the Tree of Life, great sadness in his voice. "My time has come to leave this garden, I have a greater task than training a miserable watchdog. This one has been a failure, consuming herself in fire.

Perhaps the next one will be better. It's a pity such responsibility and power is given to these vain creatures."

"It is not ours to reason why, you and I, it is just our destiny to nurture and hope. Only the worms can elect for character or as in the case of this useless creature, the lack of it. Who can question the ways of our Lords? They leave us to fulfill a mission, and as long as life continues we can only hope. Are you going to be a Guardian elsewhere?"

"No... A Lordling has come into its own and must be returned to its elders for training. It knows little of the ways and must be taught by the Lords," The Old One told his friend, the Tree of Life.

"Yes I can see the stone-one coming for you even now. You must climb into your golden ark for the stone one draws near."

"First I must finish my task at this Garden. It has been a good Garden and the fault is not yours wisest of Trees."

"Thank you for your friendship and kind words old friend," the One Tree uttered in a broken voice.

"Now I must purge this Garden and leave it free for you to continue doing--as you have before time began," the pure energy force said, in last farewell to an Elder that had permitted him to share the raising of a galaxy watchdog.

As the pure energy of the Old One swelled and filled the Garden, all within it became part of the life force itself. Soon the garden was cleansed of all... All except the Tree, and the new small green worm that hid safely high in the Tree.

The One Tree felt about the garden for traces of the Old One, but as she knew, his golden casket was gone, his duties were required elsewhere.

DERVISALS EVERYWHERE

Marples sat up and rubbed his eyes in disbelief, for the Clearing of the previous night could hardly be described as a clearing now. There was not a solitary inch in the clearing not occupied by a soldier of the dreaded Dervisal Kingdom. Even now they were busy cooking vabra grain in large black pots. Much movement was taking place in a relaxed and friendly manner. Yet none of the smells, nor any of the noises penetrated the glowing bubble encasing Rhaeve and Marples. Rhaeve sat cross legged watching Marples. "You have slept for three days," Rhaeve said, stretching, and getting to her feet in a single fluid movement.

""Why did you let me sleep?" Marples asked.

"Either I let you sleep, or I awake you to die."

"You mean that if you'd have awakened me before now, that the Dervisals would have killed me?"

"I didn't say you would be killed. I said, you would die. Your life-level was so low that you should have taken the big sleep of no return, yet you live. You are obviously of stouter material than you appear. . . Come. . We can wash at their Campfire. They have warm water and sweet soap. Come," Rhaeve said, taking his hand to guide him.

As they walked towards the cook-fires, the Dervisals melted from before them, but without fear, they just moved calmly out of the way, even as a child would have moved out of the path of a slow moving horse and wagon.

"Can they see us?" Marples asked.

"No. My Aura is impenetrable."

"Then how does air come through, and look we have just enveloped the fire and cooking utensils. If this is a force field, how come it didn't reject these objects? Look! Even the smoke is drifting normally through the bubble. How can it keep the cold from entering, yet let the smoke out? Are you sure this is not just an illusion? Or are you a magi after all?"

"Marples, Marples, you look to complicate a simple process. It is merely an envelope of elective material."

"Elective material?" Marples challenged. "I never heard of elective material." Marples challenged.

"I see... And you are the final authority concerning all things. Is this incredible knowledge restricted to Rhapour or does it encompass the whole wide universe?" Rhaeve asked politely.

"Ok, your point is made, but to ask a stupid question. Are we in a fish bowl for these Dervisals. Or does this magic bubble let us see them, and they only see the bubble."

"Remember I said it was an elective envelope. Well I am the elector, and it heeds my needs. Just like TC does for you, only the bubble is slightly more compact," Rhaeve grinned.

"And does it have the powers of thought that TC has as well?"

"No... Unlike the relationship between you and TC, I have my own brain, and it works without assistance." So saying, Rhaeve pulled Marples nose, and Marples chased her around the camp, the two of them laughing as children. The stern Dervisals on the other hand, were thrown into confusion, getting out of the way of the one-way force field that, moved erratically and very very dangerously through their camp. Fortunately none were murdered by the playing of the unthinking pair in the bubble. The fierce feline-dromedary mounts of the Dervisals hissed and spit as the bubble neared any of them, but at the last minute, realizing that they were not intimidating the glowing bubble, they too, gave way.

A squat almost toad-like Dervisal, dressed simply in a yellow robe that perfectly matched his skin coloring, approached the bubble cautiously, yet with dignity.

"I have not approached because you have not summoned me to do so, but I break our code of courtesy and do so only because you are behaving in a manner very dangerous to the troops. We have been sent to guide you to our capitol. We mean you no harm, and we see that you mean us none. But to move that glowing ball of energy indiscriminately through our camp is very dangerous to our life," the little yellow man said, embarrassed, for speaking first. "May I inquire if you are The Rhaeve?"

"Yes I am the Rhaeve of Rha, and you are?"

"I am Ghople Tsi. The unworthy voice of this miserable assortment of rascals," the small yellow man said, with quiet pride. Dignity flowed from the small man in spite of his humble words. "We have waited ever for your arrival. Some infidels have questioned your coming, but never a true believer. For are you not the light," Ghople stated, not questioned.

"I am the Rhaeve, First daughter of Light, Mother of Change, First High princess of Rha," Rhaeve spoke softly, but her voice carried for all to hear.

"It is truly Her who sees without sight," Ghople cried dropping to his knees, and then kowtowing deeply. The entire host followed the speaker's example, not so gracefully however, encumbered by their heavy armor. It was a comical sight to see these fierce warriors flopping flat on their faces in respect without a thought. Their mounts hissed softly in confusion.

Advance riders sprinted ahead to bring word of her coming, and the entire host sat around Ghople and the Light, waiting to march home to their capitol.

"Fortune will be the reward for the poor family of Ghople, who first spoke to the Wielder of Light. And I want to thank you for all my generations yet unborn. For this day will insure future tranquility for all," Ghople told Rhaeve.

"That is a nice thought Ghople, but how will I do this? I come only to awaken the Old Mother in the Forbidden Valley. I come not to govern nor bring change."

"Oh the change will be not for Dervisal. Long we have gone under the guise of being war-like and evil. Our civilization was born at the feet of an old prince. He took the Great Sleep in the Forbidden Valley. But before doing so, He set up a code that we have ever obeyed in Dervisal. These resplendent warriors have great armor, but their weapons bear only the sting of sleep."

"Even our fierce steeds have been genetically tampered with by your forefather to eat grass," Ghople said, proudly.

"These beasts eat grass?" Marples asked, in doubt.

The host stopped, in shock. How could another voice be coming from the body of the light. Sensing the deep confusion of the Dervisals, and also content that they meant no harm, Rhaeve dropped the force field.

"Bless you. You are only a child." Ghople said, in awe, not in doubt. "A beautiful wonderful child."

"Aeeeiiii!" agreed the host in one voice.

"And I know of you, companion to the Light," Ghople said.

"How do you?" asked Marples.

"We have been long instructed to present a frightening countenance to all on Rhapour, all except the Magi who lives by the glowing lake. For the old prince felt deep concern about the accident caused by his Starcruiser colliding with yours. It is written in our archives that he constantly referred to the Dragon of Forbidden Valley, as being a lazy stupid sloot and the cause of that terrible accident. All his brethren perished in the accident, and he finally went to the Big Sleep in the forbidden valley."

"Do you mean a True prince is even now sleeping in the valley of the dragon?" Rhaeve asked.

"Yes, he has been there since the very beginning of our civilization. His presence has always guided our ways," Ghople said.

"Then you have never raped and murdered?" Marples asked.

"Good gracious no," exclaimed Ghople.

"What of all the stories over the years," Marples continued.

"What of all the stories of you? And of your gorge?" replied Ghople, a trace of humor in his otherwise toneless voice. "Not only is there a parallel—It seems the prince copied your system. It is in our archives if you wish to see for yourself. Apparently he thought it an odd approach for a human to take."

"And what does that mean?" Marples challenged.

"Well it would appear to me that the prince considered your race to be warlike and very savage," replied Ghople.

"Ghople is right Marples. I spent three days with TC studying your history, and it is not one to be proud of," Rhaeve put in in the defense of Ghople. Ghople smiled his thanks to Rhaeve. He was not enjoying talking to this aggressive human and was glad that Rhaeve had taken his side.

"As a matter of fact Marples, I have considered how a race such as yours could have ever evolved without destroying the very planet it occupies. Even as we speak, it is no longer a planet that you would be familiar with. When I return to my galaxy I have every intention of recommending your galaxy be appointed a young watchdog," Rhaeve told Marples hotly.

"What!" Marples howled.

"You heard me. I see that deep in your past an explorer was wrecked upon your planet. Apparently by what

I can deduce, the Lord of the pyramind was wrecked by the pyramind landing on top of him in a long green valley. Well it seems the upside-down landing of the pyramind turned the valley to waste desert where even today nothing grows. The crew and passengers were all disabled and died soon thereafter. Only one of the energy producing Old Ones remained active for awhile, trying to establish some sort of linking between the dying survivors and the local savages. Necessity forced the Old One to take his sick and dying passengers to the mountains so that he could protect them from the savages. Apparently to no avail. The Old One had only energy to work with and very little genetic understanding. It could be that I have not pieced the puzzle together entirely accurate, but then I am only making my supposition based on information found in the brain of TC."

"Whaaaa... " Marples said, his mind barely grasping the implications of Rhaeve's outburst.

"In the long history of your planet, there was no atomic powered civilization, in your past, no technologies existed, no dragons, yet your religions spoke of demons and unknown powers that were clearly atomic, having been in existence. All of your religions tell of happenings not recorded factually. Only in the minds-eye of religions. I find no other acceptable conclusion than that of a deep space exploration probe being stranded on your planet," Rhaeve concluded.

"If that is the case, what became of the Energy that is known as an Old One?" Marples asked sincerely.

"Probably realizing that he could only bring death to all he encountered he gave them what laws and help he could, then he projected into your sun and became once more a part of his birth."

Marples just sat down and shook his head.

"TC has described in detail an upside-down pyramind, with its power-base facing the sky and it's top laying flat on the scorched sand of what remains of a very weak atomic happening."

"But we have many pyraminds in the desert. They can't all be Starships." Marples said.

"None of the great stone ones are. Soon you will see a true Pyramind, as created by a Rhanian Lord," Rhaeve told Marples.

Sensing that Rhaeve was ready to travel, Ghople signaled for the Company to move out. Ghople-the-poor, was on foot. All the other golden warriors rode a huge beast of war, that could have been very dangerous, if not held in control by its rider. Rhaeve speculated as why the voice of such a huge war party would be on foot.

As they headed away from the Shadow into the heartland of the Dervisal, the land became steadily more inhospitable and only the feldro was at home. Rhaeve felt this war-mount would be at home regardless of the terrain. Ghople wished that his personal feldro was under him, but that would have left his guest to be foot. Propriety would forbid such a breach in manners, and he the voice could receive no better passage than he could afford his anticipated guest. And to expect a feldro to permit any than it's personal friend to mount it was insane.

On aching feet the threesome walked for five days, Ghople thought a cart would have been nice, if only a feldro would pull one. With aching feet, Ghople-the-poor, voice of all Dervisal, asked the company to halt for the night. "Tomorrow we should reach Darva, and a bath," he told his guests.

"Are you the only speaker in this war party?" Marples asked.

"Yes for it is a useless thing to learn all the languages of Rhapour, and only one of little worth could be spared for the long training," Ghople said, sitting cross legged and examining his raw feet.

"What of those that trade with the Nodites?" Marples asked.

"They are traders, and learn what they need to trade."

"Here, let my examine your feet," Rhaeve told Ghople, quickly kneeling and taking an uncallused foot in her hand Rhaeve looked deep into his soft brown eyes. Rhaeve could feel the pain, even there. "This is terrible! You are smooth of foot, why do I feel that you have never walked so far in your entire life?"

"True... I am not accustomed to walking. I spend much time at my worthless studies, preparing myself to greet those who speak not our language."

"Why do you call your studies worthless?" Rhaeve asked, now holding both of his feet in her small strong hands.

"Trouble yourself not about me, for I am merely the unworthy servant to these fine young men," Ghople said, trying to extract his feet from the tight grip of the child without offending her.

"How far is the Forbidden Valley from Darva?" Rhaeve asked, letting go of Ghople's feet, and effortlessly rising to her own.

"Only two days slow march," Ghople said, wriggling his toes.

"I feel no pain," Ghople said, in a voice filled with thanks.

"And you never should have," Rhaeve replied angrily. "Take my hand," Rhaeve commanded, helping Ghople to his feet.

"Aeeeyahhhhh!" the golden warriors cried as one being, throwing themselves once more to the ground in a golden splash of respect.

"They are going to damage themselves if they continue flopping on the ground like that," Marples said, to Rhaeve.

"It's their custom of showing respect. And if you think I am going to tamper with customs that aren't dangerous to life you have learned nothing from our being together."

"Angry words do not hide a kind deed," Marples grinned.

That night while eating her simple vabra grain meal with Marples and the humble voice of all Dervisals, Rhaeve watched the warriors happily polishing their golden armor.

"Strange warriors. They feed on grain, and sing happy songs without drinking, fighting, wenching," Marples said, to Ghople...

"It's only because they are truly simple farmers who play at war. Never a life has been taken in our land. Even the smallest creature has a right to life," Ghople replied simply.

"Then you eat no meat?' Marples asked.

"No!" Ghople said, as if he was dislodging a dirty object from his throat. "We have not the right to eat our humble little brothers, though they be animal or fish, for in all life the greatest of us must be no more than the weakest."

"Does that mean then that even the humblest of your kind could not be the greatest," Marples asked.

"I suppose. . . . " Ghople said with a twinkle in his otherwise unfathomable soft brown eyes. "But now we should sleep, for soon comes the light, and a full day of walking."

THE GATHERING

In the morning, after a leisure breakfast of grains, cooked in a manner to excite even the most jaded of pallets, they were ready to travel.

"How are your feet this fine morning Ghople?" Rhaeve asked, mischievously, showing small white teeth.

"Fine. You truly have the touch that is told only the Lords of Rha have."

"Do you plan on continuing with this masquerade?" Rhaeve asked Ghople.

"Masquerade?" came the strangled reply from Ghople.

"Certainly it is a masquerade for us to be expected to believe that you are the humble servant of all these farmers."

"But I truly am their servant," Ghople sputtered.

"And you are not the leader of all present?" Rhaeve continued doggedly.

"Not in the way you mean. I am merely the voice that has the ability to speak of what it sees," Ghople protested.

"Then you are of authority!" Rhaeve fired at him.

"If I speak of what I see, and if they are kind enough to listen, then I am flattered," Ghople said, simply.

"Would I be wrong in presuming that you speak for all of Dervisal. Are you not the leader of all this land?"

"I have been listened to by many, as I am old, but I rule no man. On occasion I have had the privilege to speak to all my fellow Dervisals. And on even rarer occasions, they have all listened to my voice. It has been a great blessing to my humble family," Ghople said, gently, as if reproaching a small child.

"My god! He is the king.... We have a king for our guide," Marples exclaimed.

"No... He is as he claims. He is the servant of all his people. It is a fine concept, and I will give it considerable thought. For I see that many of our watch dogs could learn much from this simple man," Rhaeve told Marples.

Rhaeve walked over to the first snarling feldro in the line. As Rhaeve approached the beast, the snarling became a mewling, and then a deep contented purring. Rhaeve reached up and took it's velvety muzzle in her small hand, and immediately the feldro sat on its haunches in a position for a rider to mount.

"He will carry you as well as his present rider, and I see that he has asked two more of his friends to accept Marples and myself," Rhaeve told Ghople.

"How? They have never accepted other than their one rider."

"Have you ever asked them?" asked Rhaeve

"No, we have always assumed that they would become angry, so we never asked it of them," Ghople said.

"Come let us go, for in ten days I must be in the valley, for only then will the black hole be open."

On foot, and alone, Rhaeve left the city of Darva. Marples had to be given a strong mental command to stop him from following. Rhaeve had to go alone, as the Forbidden Valley was well named. As she approached the dish of molten rock that was called the Forbidden Valley, she notice skeletons of those that had entered, only to stumble back out and die of heavy radiation.

In the very center of the small valley a great blue pyramind lay buried with its tip buried in the molten rock, the flat base was facing the stars. A stone ramp had been piled to form a road leading to the top. Rhaeve noticed as she climbed the long ramp, that the crater around the ramp held many bones. On each corner of the pyramind sat a gray stone troll, each holding a golden coffin. Rhaeve walked across to the nearest one. A dim glow was emanating from within. Rhaeve walked the three hundred feet to the next coffin, again a dim glow greeted her from within, the next was the same, only a dim glow. The last casket glowed strongly, and Rhaeve could not help but notice that these coffins were all identical, and she also noticed that they were identical to the descriptions in TC's memory banks..... of the ark on earth. She would investigate it later.

The entire center of the platform was taken up by the curled body of the sleeping dragon.

"She sure is big isn't she?" a musical voice came from the open mouth of the dragon...

"Is it the Great Blue Troll?" Rhaeve asked, knowing that only the troll could have brought the remaining casket to its corner position on the pyramind. No other being was powerful enough to haul a golden casket filled with the incredible mass of even a very weak Old One. And one as active as the brightly glowing casket held enough radiation to scour the planet if released. Only a stone troll could manage the job.

"Who else," Blewitt said, stepping into view.

"You are so small!" blurted Rhaeve, before she thought of what she was saying.

"Good things come in small packages," Blewitt said, good naturedly, "and you aint exactly a giant yourself. Kind of pretty for a humanoid. .. Too bad you wasn't a troll-lady. We could have a trip home to make the stars sit up and take notice."

"You're a cheeky little fellow for sure," Rhaeve said, pretending to be cross. "Somehow I always pictured trolls to be like those gigantic stone monoliths holding the engines."

"Yup, that's the general attitude, but as trolls go I'm the biggest in all the known galaxies, and the most powerful, if I must modestly say," Blewitt said, reaching around with his incredibly long arms and patting himself on the back.

"Well as braggarts go, you are certainly the greatest I've ever met, but I suppose that if you could haul all four of these caskets up here you must have more energy than you appear to."

"Yup I does, but right now it's your turn to do your stuff. That is if you know the way home for openers" Blewitt said, giving Rhaeve a rude wink. They both laughed.

"If all the trolls are like you, they have been named wrong."

"What kind of name would you have given us Princess?" Blewitt said, running a yellow tongue across his orange lips.

"Imps…. Yes definitely Imps," Rhaeve said, laughing as Blewitt combed his thick eyebrows with his webbed fingers.

"Well let's get the show on the road. Did you get the co-ordinates from Thragg?" Blewitt asked, getting serious.

"Certainly. Otherwise we would be just about to head out for an eternity in the deep."

Overhead the sun was just reaching its daily zenith as Rhaeve climbed to the head of the dragon. "Get in her mouth, I'm going to activate one engine at a time, even so it will be just a trifle hot. . . Even for the biggest troll ever," Rhaeve laughed.

Satisfied that the troll was deep within the bowels of the dragon, Rhaeve opened both of her golden eyes. She slowly started to glow blue-white, her color matching that of the pyramind. Sparks cascaded down across the back of the sleeping dragon. Soon the dust of thousands of years incinerated itself and the dragons plates took on a soft yellow glow.

Deep in the belly of the dragon, the troll felt life returning to the Sky

Queen. Beside the troll, the sleeping prince stirred for the first time since the prince had crawled into the life preserving belly of the dragon. Green life-blood coursed slowly through long unused organs.

Rhaeve had already fired up engine number one, and that ark was now itself drawing energy from the nearest star. Content that it was stable and building energy, Rhaeve blasted a hard-drive message to the troll, "move number one engine to minus six degrees. I'm going to lock it onto a different star. I don't want it sapping the one it's on".

"I'm going to try and fire all four engines up with this star, and I don't want to overload it. Stay on line, as I'm about to fire up number two engine."

Again her eyes blazed at a golden casket, energy beaming down into Rhaeve and blazing out at the sleeping energy-being. Shortly, a dim light connecting it to the star the first ark had previously been locked on.

Soon a blue-white arc was connecting the star and ark-engine.

Correcting co-ordinates were fed to the troll and shortly all four engines had the sky ablaze with lines of power flowing from four different stars to the engines. The plates on the dragon were humming with blue light, and two great eyes opened slowly.

Rhaeve started to give the dragon instructions of flight as the great pyramind itself slowly absorbed the incredible energy coming in from the four engines.

Suddenly the sky was normal on Rhapour. And the Forbidden Valley was empty of all life. Only the hard radiation remained.

A NEW GARDEN

Circle mind-felt about her. She knew she was in a different time already. The garden grew in her mind. It whirled and swirled and engulfed her mind. Soon the Garden grew lush and ready for her new charge. Up into her magnificent boughs of safety crawled a small green snake. It crawled high into the greenest foliage for protection. It was a small snake, hardly more than a worm. It was her snake, and Circle knew that she must nurture and protect it until it had the right to leave her garden. It was a good garden, and Circle felt good about this small one.

"I am to be your guide, your teacher, and your guardian. I will be your keeper until I know you are mature enough to go from this garden and find your way Come down and see this wonderful garden that was created just for you."

"Where am I?" asked a small gentle voice.

"Eden," came a whisper from the garden itself.

"Who are you?" the small defenseless snake asked in abject fear, "and who am I?" it continued politely.

"Never mind that for now. Come look into this clear pool, and we will see who you may become . . . I will call you Circe. . .For a long long time... Let us hope you grow tall in mind. And sing sweet songs... As only you can. Come sit," the Tree of Life said, dropping a small pebble into the clear pond.

"Come sit and watch this circle of circles, as it continues forever -- My little friend," the Tree said, rustling its leaves happily in hope of a new tomorrow.

"What is Forever, Old One?" asked the young serpent.

And the unbroken circle of change began again...

As it had FOREVER……………

"THE END"